SALLY

A WOMAN OF HER TIME

KATHERINE JANE

Published by Katherine Jane

ISBN: 978-1-7642070-0-3 (paperback)

FIRST LARGE PRINT EDITION, 2025

For book orders and enquiries, contact:
katherinejaneauthor@gmail.com

Instagram: katherinejaneauthor
Facebook: katherinejaneauthor

A catalogue record for this book is available from the National Library of Australia

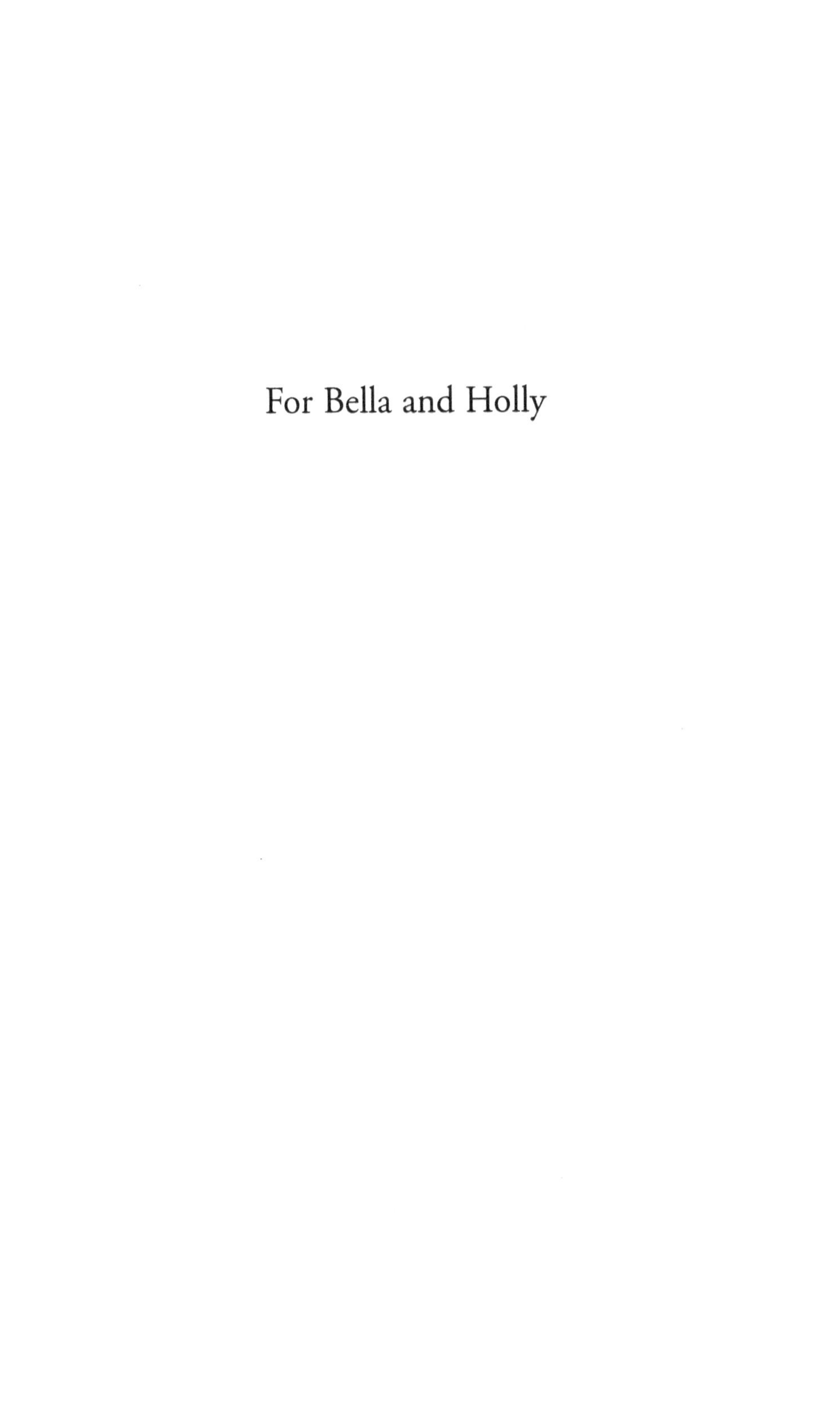

For Bella and Holly

Preface

Ever since Sally told me that she and Jack met for the first time when she was only six years old and Jack was a lad of eighteen, I knew there was a story to be told. So I made it up. Well, most of it anyway. Sally was in her eighties when she started to talk about her past, and there was not a lot of information passed on to me. I had known her for quite some time before she opened up to me. But I didn't have a chance to write this story until I had retired. So, where to get more information? I knew Sally's children quite well, and was in contact with them all, so I asked them for help with some of the time line. I have changed their names of course, but they will recognise themselves.

This is a story about a real woman of her time and her lifetime love. It is also the story of the children she and her husband produced. Though much of it is pure fiction, it could have happened this way.

Enjoy.

CHAPTER 1

Minnipa SA, 1929

Meredith hated Mondays. Monday was washing day and she had to help her mother with the family wash. Rain, hail or shine. Not that it rained a lot on the farm and she didn't really know what hail was. But the worst thing was that she was not allowed to go to school on Monday because it was washing day. Meredith was six years old and had only just started school at the beginning of the year. She loved it. This particular Monday was fine and sunny which meant that all the washing would dry and they would have nice clean sheets on their beds tonight. If it did rain, on a Monday, well, the chances of sleeping between prickly blankets was pretty high. The family really only had one set of sheets for every bed. It was only the generosity of her father's sisters, Aunty E and Aunty G, that they ever got new linen. Any old sheets of course, were cut down for cot sheets for the baby or made into every day table cloths, pyjamas for the children, and the worst of the worn parts became cleaning cloths.

Meredith kept pushing on the handle of the big wringer while her mother fed the sheets through. She was tall for her age and quite clever (she had been told this at school, not by her parents) so was enlisted by her mother to help with the washing every Monday. School was not a priority for a girl anyway. Pretty soon the wash basket was full and she took one side, her mother the other, and they carried the heavy basket off the veranda to the line behind the farmhouse.

The house was still quite new. Meredith's father, David Chandler, had built the house the year that Meredith was born. That is to say, he had it built. It was made of the local stone quarried in the area. Two bedrooms, a kitchen, sitting room and a separate dining room. Veranda on all four sides. The bathroom and laundry were in an enclosed veranda at the back. The toilet was quite separate to the main house. Plumbing in those days was very basic. All inside drains simply ended in the garden area. There was a septic pit, but the "dunny" pans still had to be emptied manually. All in all, it was a very sturdy house. Having a separate dining room was quite an exception for the time, and was Meredith's mother's pride and joy. The whole project had been funded by David's family back in Adelaide.

It was when Meredith was handing up washing from the second basket for the day that she saw her father talking to someone on the side veranda. A stranger. He was tall, almost as tall as her father and quite skinny. He had really dark hair and was holding a pipe in his hand. She couldn't see his face but knew he was a stranger. The only other person she knew who smoked a pipe was Willy-Jack, the old Aboriginal man who lived in his humpy in the middle of the oats paddock. Why Willy Jack was allowed to live there was never explained to her. But she had sometimes seen her father squatting down near Willy-Jack and talking to him. She thought they were probably friends. She knew it was very unusual for a farmer to be friends with an Aborigine. And apparently it was very unusual for an Aborigine to smoke a pipe. Meredith didn't understand a lot things and although she wanted explanations, she knew better than to ask too many questions. A six year old girl was only told what she needed to know to help with her younger brothers, help with the washing, help with the chickens, help with practically anything that she was big enough to do.

'Who's that talking to dad?' she tentatively asked her mother.

'Don't know.' Replied her mother. 'Probably someone looking for work. Hand up that next thing Meredith and just concentrate on what you're doing.'

Later that day, when the washing was all brought in, the baby was having a nap and Peter, the four year old, was playing mud pies in the vegetable patch behind the house, Meredith snuck off across the fenced off house yard, to go and see the horses in their yard behind the "Big" shed. It was referred to as the "Big" shed because it housed the old Bedford truck, the plough used to prepare the paddocks for wheat, barley and oat planting, a feed room which stored food for the horses and chooks, a lot of fencing stuff, the saddles and other tack for the two horses and all sorts of other farming things that her father used, or no longer used. There was also a small room with a bed and an old wood stove that was used as living quarters for any farm hands who came through. There had been three so far that Meredith remembered, and she didn't pay them much attention. No doubt there would be others. They didn't seem to stay long.

The two horses sensed her coming and trotted over to the fence and whinnied softly while Meredith took it in turns scratching one long ear then another. She had plucked some long grass from near the tank stand on her way across the yard and was feeding this to the horses. They seemed to relish it.

'G'day.' Meredith heard. The fella who had been talking to her father was standing a few feet away. She had not heard him approach. She did not reply. Just kept feeding the horses the grass she had brought over. She could see him from the corner of her eye. He was really tall, and really skinny. He was not a proper man yet but not a kid either. He had that pipe in his hand still and could do with a shave.

'Nice nags. Have you got your own pony?' No reply. 'I used to have a pony.' The man/boy continued. 'Pretty little thing. I used to ride up and down the rows in an orchard near where I lived as a kid. Up and down the rows all day on that pony and I would shoot off a round of shot every five minutes or so. It was to keep the birds away from the fruit trees. I got paid one shilling a week. That was my first job out of school. I was only twelve at the time. I'm eighteen now.' Still no response.

'So what's your name? I'm Jack by the way.' Meredith thought he was alright, but she wasn't supposed to talk to the farmhands, which she supposed he was going to be. She quietly moved off from the fence, head down, to walk back to the house.

'If you don't tell me your name I'm going to call you Sally.' He called after her. But he didn't move to follow her. Meredith skipped away. She liked the name and she liked the fella. Not much made her skip these days and she caught herself, and slowed down to a walk.

That night, at tea time, everyone sat around the rough kitchen table. The dining room was reserved for visitors. Her mother, Mabel and father David, little Peter sitting on cushions on a chair and the baby Charlie was in a high chair of sorts. Something David had put together for Meredith when she was a little-one. It was rickety, but still held together. Jack was there too. That confirmed that he was a new farmhand. The farmhands slept in the shed, but had three meals a day with the family. There was some Government scheme which sent the young unemployed men off to farms and they subsidised the small wages the farmers paid. Meredith didn't know much about the finances of such things, but she understood that money was always short.

'This is Jack'. David said, nodding toward the young man. 'He'll be helping us out for a little while.' Everyone went quiet. They had been through this before. The farmhands came and then left. The farm was not profitable and yields barely provided enough money to buy the family the few essentials they needed. The weather and soil of the west coast of South Australia was very limited in its favours. Besides, the soldier settlers who came there really had no idea what they were doing. A bit of book learning didn't really teach them much. The more successful farmers had money behind them and could afford to take risks. David could not. He nodded around the table at each person introducing 'The Misses, Young Peter, the baby of the family we call Charlie and Meredith.'

'Oh I've met Sally.' The young man grinned. Meredith dropped her fork. Her head went straight down and she knew she was blushing. She was not supposed to talk to the farmhands and now this one, this nice one, would get her into trouble.

'Sally?' said her mother, looking at the young man and then frowning at the girl. 'I quite like that name. I used to have a friend called Sally.'

Life seemed just that little bit nicer for the next few months for Sally. All the family called her Sally now. She was still Meredith at school, but at home she was Sally and no-one made any comment on the name. She was very careful not to approach Jack when she saw him, but didn't shy away quite so much when he spoke to her. She somehow felt as if she was recognised as a person by this farmhand. She was not just someone to do chores on the farm. She felt like she was a person in her own right. But of course, it was hard for a six year old to comprehend this. She didn't mind missing school on Mondays like she used to and would help her mother get through the washing as quick as possible. There were always other chores to do, even on school days. Something changed in her though. She started to appreciate those chores. She got to like the chickens and named each one of them. She helped her mother in the veggie patch and actually paid attention when her mum tried to teach her something about the garden. She even gladly helped Peter make his mud pies. She was only a kid herself, surely she could play in the mud too?

Occasionally, she would take Peter out to visit Willy-Jack at his wurlie in the middle of the oats paddock. The children would squat down on the ground and just wait for Willy Jack to come out of his humpy. The wurlie was made of branches and bark and sort of leaned against an old mallee tree. One of the few remaining trees in the paddocks set aside for cropping. The land in the Minnipa area of the Eyre Peninsular was by no means lush. There had been grazing in the past, but most of those early settlers walked off the land and gave up their lease holdings. The mallee grew sporadically where it could along the creek lines. There were huge granite rocks which rose up above the ground like sleeping giants. The largest of these in the area Tcharkuldu Rock, was on the family holding. David complained that it took up about a quarter of his land. But it was a good source of water because when it did rain, which was not often, the water poured off the rock and made multiple little streams which spread across the farm.

Willy-Jack told the children the dream time story of how the rocks were formed. The story was lost on Peter, and Sally didn't quite understand about the great spirits, but in time she learned to appreciate the stories Willy-Jack told her. The old man didn't talk much about day to day happenings or anything that seemed to relate to the present time. But one day he said. 'Him leaving soon.'

'Who?' asked Sally. But she knew who he meant. Willy-Jack hardly ever commented on everyday events, and when he did, it was these short, disjointed sentences.

'That tall fella. But he come back someday.'

Sally didn't question him. She had been told not to listen too much to what Willy-Jack said. Her father was the only person who was supposed to have any contact with him, so Sally just pretended she didn't know what he was talking about, or didn't care much.

A week after that last visit to Willy-Jack, Jack left. David told him there was no further need for a farm-hand during summer. The crop was harvested and there was not much work to be done. The young man was expecting this outcome, so said his polite good buys to David and The Misses and cuffed young Peter gently under the chin. He didn't say anything to Sally, just nodded and gave her a wink when he turned to go. He strode off across the yard with his swag over his shoulder, heading for the main road into town. Sally was the only one in the family who continued to watch him walk away. She wanted to run after him. Her chest hurt, but she didn't really know why. She liked this farmhand. She had hardly spoken to him, but she knew she liked him. Instead, she stood rooted to the ground. While she watched, the young man half turned toward her and waved, holding his pipe up high. 'I'll be back Sally. Don't you worry 'bout that.'

CHAPTER 2

1930-1937

The boys were growing up and soon there were the three of them going to school in Minnipa. The town was only about four miles from the farm but still too far to walk, especially for Charlie. When little Charlie started school Sally was already twelve and in Grade 7. The three of them used to ride the old draft horse into town. The mare was about twenty four years old and steady as a rock. David had bought another horse to pull the plough but kept old Jessy for emergencies and to act as the school bus. In town she was stabled in a lean-too at the school along with other assorted livestock. There was by now a pony on the farm, as well as the other work horse. The pony was supposed to be for all the children to learn to ride, but the only one it would let mount her was Sally.

Feisty little thing but Sally loved her. After much coaching from Sally the pony eventually permitted the boys to mount and Sally taught them to ride. They could only ride the pony, however, when Sally was leading her. Otherwise, the minute the boy was seated, off she would go, tearing around the paddock. It wore Sally out chasing the horse, but she was chuffed to know that the pony would only obey her. Old Jessy was a much more reliable animal and was content to have three children on her back. No saddle of course.

There was more to the children's education than the little one room school in town. Neither parent was well educated but they did have a range of practical skills. As much as possible, these were passed on to the children. David was always struggling with the farm work so he co-opted the children in whenever he could. His own agricultural skills were somewhat lacking, however he did the best he could. There was only ever one growing season on the West Coast and that was during winter. So once the crops were harvested, he used to buy in a few sheep. It took him a few years to realise that if he wanted the sheep to only graze the stubble and whatever other vegetation was around, he had to not buy too many. Otherwise, they required hand feeding with feed which he could not afford, or they died. And of course, having grazing animals meant the fencing had to be constantly maintained. The stock also needed water. It was not an easy life for David and some of the other Soldier Settler farmers. Really, they had no idea what they were doing. The Government should not have sent them out to those marginal areas. Apparently the motivation of the Government was to populate the rural areas. Rail lines were built. Water supplies established. In fact, Tcharkuldu Rock, on David's farm was turned into the towns water supply. The government built a concrete wall around the base of the rock and directed the rain fall catchment to the town by way of a concrete channel. There were some years, when the small leasing fee for this rock was the major income for the family. There were years when there was not enough rain to siphon off for the stock. Then there were years when the sheep died and the crops failed for whatever reason. Sheep, if they thrived, had to be shorn and shearers were expensive. That was another skill David had to learn. He learnt how to slaughter sheep for the family pantry. He learnt how to shoe the horses and trim their hooves. His only seeding equipment was a horse drawn plough. Harvesting was done by hand. Some of the larger, and wealthier farmers were looking at steam driven combine harvesters.

But that was way out David's range. After the reaping, there was threshing and then winnowing. And finally, the grain had to be hand bagged and driven to the rail terminal. That work horse sure earnt its feed every day.

David also learnt how to drink and he learnt how to gamble.

There was very little money, and Mabel had to try to make up the difference in any way she could. These two had a strange relationship. Well, probably not for the times. They seemed to communicate well enough, but few words were actually spoken between them. There was absolutely no signs of affection. In the quiet of the evening, when all work was done, David would sit staring into the fire and Mabel would sit knitting or darning or mending. Sally supposed there was contentment there, but not much else. Mabel had the usual domestic skills of gardening, cooking, knitting, sewing etc. These all became Sally's staple duties once she had mastered them. But there was one skill Mabel had which afforded an extra income for the family. She was an accomplished pianist.

Over the years, the population of Minnipa increased. So much so, that quite a social network developed. There was the golf club and the tennis club. Courts were built near both local churches and church halls erected.

Both the Catholic and the Anglican Church had their own piano and a little stage in their respective halls. Mabel began teaching piano lessons in the Anglican hall. Once a week she would drive the truck into town for supplies and spend the afternoon at the Church Hall teaching whatever locals could afford for her lessons. Cash was not necessary. The old barter system worked well. It did not bring in a lot of money, but it did help the family's position. Getting into town on a regular basis still had to meet with David's approval, but for the most part he conceded. He knew that the money was needed. Mabel didn't mind driving during the day, but refused at night time. The kangaroos and rabbits trying to cross the road was just too much to bear. Eventually, Saturday night dances started. Mabel's reputation was such that she was co-opted into a small dance band. Basically, anyone who could play an instrument took their turn in the band. But the musicians did get paid. Mabel was the mainstay of the local band and they were often asked to play at other nearby towns. The old jalopy that David had somehow acquired got a good workout ferrying the band around to various engagements. Sally was left in charge of her brothers while her mother was off performing. In David's case, drinking, and if there was any chance of a game, a little wager.

When Peter turned twelve and was in Grade 7, arrangements were made for him to go to high school in Adelaide, over 350 miles away. One of Mabel's sisters paid for the boy's education. David's two maiden sisters lived in the family home in Eden Hills in the Adelaide hills. So it was there that Peter lived whilst attending high school.

These arrangements were made with no input from the children. The school at Minnipa only went as far as grade 7. There was no local high school on the whole of the peninsular. Sally, who was approaching fourteen had repeated grade 7 twice simply because she had to wait to reach the legal age for children to leave school. She was never offered high school by her parents. She was expected to stay at the local school until she turned fourteen and then help out on the farm and looking after her youngest brother. When she heard the news, Sally just wanted to go to her room and cry. Her throat hurt and her stomach twisted. It wasn't jealousy as such, she loved her brother, but what about her education? She didn't cry of course, she had to pretend that this was a good thing for Peter. And it was, but

Sally had wanted to be an architect. She was an excellent scholar and felt she deserved the chance of higher education. But, she was a girl and, in her parents' eyes, not worthy of the expense. Not that they could afford it of course. The hardest thing for Sally was that her parents didn't think she was worthy of even trying to educate past grade seven. It was just expected of her that she stay on the farm. Only boys were worth an education. If Sally had not already felt like a second class citizen, she certainly did now.

Still, she did like the rural life. Once she left school and was able to join the golf and tennis clubs, she discovered that she was very good at both sports. The farm was faltering more and more so her mother put more and more effort into her musical endeavours. David spent a lot of time visiting his sisters in Adelaide. It was thought the reason for this was to keep in touch with Peter. In fact, both parents seemed to spend more and more time away from home. She became responsible for Charlie most of the time and so much more of the general farm management was up to her. She was quite capable of these extra responsibilities, but did hope that she would occasionally get thanked for her work. She did not.

There was some reprieve for Sally during the school holidays. She was often sent to Adelaide to stay with her two aunts in the big house in the hills. Sometimes her mother came with her and sometimes it was her father. But never both at the same time. The trip to Adelaide was quite arduous. It was usually by train, which took two days. Occasionally a train trip to the coast and then by ship up to Port Adelaide. The sea travel always made her sick, but she knew it was no use complaining. Once in the city, there was another train trip through the hills to get to the house. No one owned a motor car in her family. The old jalopy that David used at the farm would never have made the distance.

The house in Eden Hills was grand. It had been built by David's grandparents in 1915. David's grandfather was a successful business owner in Adelaide. The origins of the family went back to the first free settlers ship from England. The family came with a bit of money behind them and successive generations managed quite well in their chosen professions or trades. That was until David took up farming. Still, it was a lovely house with views over the city of Adelaide. There was quite a bit of land which was gradually sold off to support David's two sisters, who never married. The house was really too large for them once their parents had passed and David and Mabel moved to Minnipa. So the lower level was turned into a kind of self contained flat which the sisters rented out to bring in a bit more money.

All three children loved that house. Charlie was always finding new places to hide in the sprawling gardens. Peter liked to set up a hammock across one of the four veranda corners. He would swing there for hours reading. Sally just loved the grandeur of it all. She used to pretend she was lady of the manor. She had a lot less responsibility here in this big house and could indulge her fantasies of being a wealthy land owner. Never a wealthy land owner's wife. In her daydreams Sally was the station owner and boss.

It was during one of these stays with the aunts that Sally made a friendship with a girl she met at church in Eden Hills. This friendship was to last a lifetime. The two girls could have been like twins. Not identical twins, it was nothing to do with their looks. They thought about things the same way, they liked the same kind of books, they both played the piano, liked sport. They just clicked. The relationship made with her friend Josie, and her family, proved to be very significant as Sally entered adulthood and continued throughout her life. With the Wright family she felt valued as a person. There had been that farmhand from years ago, when she was a little kid, but he was long gone.

CHAPTER 3

1937

Back at the farm, things were going from bad to worse. For two years in a row, the aunts had sent money to David's family to see them through. At least now he could afford some seasonal farmhands to help with the harvest. This was still being done by hand. The farm was 1500 acres. But taking out the area of Tcharkuldu Rock and then the swamp land near it, there was probably less than 1000 acres of arable land. Not all of that was seeded, because of trees and creeks and goodness know what other obstacles. Even so, there was a lot of wheat and oats to be cut by hand.

Now that she had left school, Sally noted a very slight change in attitude toward her by the locals in the town. They seemed to treat her more like an adult than a child. She had joined the Anglican tennis club and was invited to compete in the under eighteens. I don't mind, she thought, even though some of the girls were two or three years older than her. But some of those girls minded, because Sally was very good and quickly became a local champion.

She joined the golf club too. Initially going there with her parents, but it just didn't seem to stick for them. It was up to her father to take her everywhere. He was becoming more and more unreliable, so she would end up riding her pony to the weekend events. Charlie often sitting behind her as she trotted into town. The same thing happened at golf. She was junior women's champion at fifteen years of age. Sally was simply a very independent and talented girl. She was shy, but still confident in her own abilities. It was only talking to other people that was difficult.

She had noticed over the past year that a tension was growing between her parents. They had never been an affectionate couple. Not like Josie's parents in Eden Hills, Mr & Mrs Wright. They were always patting each other on the hand and calling each other "dear". None of that in her family. But there was something uncomfortable going on with her parents. She couldn't quite put her finger on it.

Why did David go to Adelaide so often by himself? The farm needed him. It was a two day trip there and two or three days back depending on the trains. So he would be away two weeks at a time. Sure, once the grains had been harvested there was a six month gap before seeding. But there were always things that needed doing. He even disappeared during the growing season a few times.

And then there was her mother. Mabel seemed more interested in playing in the dance band than she did in her own family. She had taught Sally all the necessary domestic skills to manage the family. She had also taught her to play the piano, but Sally was a little short of practice time. If David was not around to take his wife to the dances, she would get a ride with other band members. One in particular seemed to show up a lot. He played the violin. Nice chap, but the way that Mabel looked at him was just a bit strange. Mabel didn't smile very often, but she always had a smile for Reginald.

Sally felt that she was holding the family and the farm together. And she was not yet fifteen years old.

It happened on a Monday, soon after Sally had left school having reached the legal age to do so. She was hanging out the washing and she heard her father talking to someone on the side veranda. She looked up from the clothes line expecting to see some new stranger sent to help her father with the harvest. She recognised the pipe first of all. It was Jack. Jack had come back.

CHAPTER 4

1937-1938

'He's back' Sally murmured to herself. It was all she could do not to drop the clean sheet she was hanging up and run up to him. 'He said he'd come back and now he's here. Oh Lord, please let him stay longer than six months this time.' No one could hear her of course. She would have turned scarlet if anyone had. Instead, she casually finished hanging out the clothes and walked back to the house, heading for the lean- to laundry. She didn't even look up as she passed where Jack and her father were standing. But she felt him look at her. She could feel the hairs on the back of her neck creep. She almost tripped over the veranda step as she entered the laundry. As soon as she thought she was alone, the biggest grin came over her face. She sat down on the overturned laundry tub which had been draining onto the floor. It took a while for her heart to stop thumping in her chest. Why was her body behaving like this? She thought. But she knew why, it was the sight of him. That straight black hair. That tall slim shape, and that infernal pipe which never left his hand. He was beautiful.

Dinner that night was excruciating. Sally kept her head down more than usual. She was so scared that if she looked up she would see him looking at her. But Jack kept up a light hearted chat with her parents and Charlie. Sort of a summary on what had happened during the past eight years. Jack had spent quite a bit of time in Port Lincoln with the fishing boats, and then a stint on farms on the other side of Adelaide.

'And I guess you've left school by now Sally?' he said at one point. She didn't respond. She didn't have to. Her mother was only too happy to fill in the gaps, uninteresting as they were, in Sally's life.

The family had acquired a house cow a couple of years previous. No one knew where it came from. David just turned up with this big Jersey on a lead line one Sunday morning. Sally suspected that he had won it at cards the previous night, but she would never say so. It was by no means cattle country on Eyre Peninsular, but some farmers kept a "house cow". Now the Chandler family had one too. Mabel had no idea what to do with it, although, fresh milk would come in very handy and make a nice change from the powdered stuff the family lived on. So Sally asked advice from her school friends who had a cow or two and soon learnt the art of milking. And yes, the fresh milk was delicious and there was plenty of it. The cow was confined to the stable yard and hand fed. When there was enough of it, Sally would gather up grass from around the tank stand for Daisy. There were also weeds pulled from the vegetable garden. Not a very original name for the cow, but it kind of stuck.

The problem now for Sally though, was that Daisy was stabled next to her pony in the same shed that the farmworkers had their living quarters. Which meant she would probably see Jack every morning. Well it wasn't really a problem, but the same rules still applied. The children were not to talk to the farmhands unless absolutely necessary. And she knew Jack would talk to her. She could not be so rude as to never respond. Besides, she wanted to talk to this man. Yes, he was a man now. She calculated that he would be around twenty seven years old. At that age he should be married with a couple of kids. She would have to find out about that.

The next morning Sally went to milk Daisy. No Jack appeared. The same the next day and the next. At first Sally didn't know whether to be disappointed or relieved. She couldn't explain it to herself, but by day three, she was definitely disappointed. The only time she saw him was at dinner time. Little conversation was entered into by any of the family now that they had all got used to this farmhand being part of the scene. David would sometimes mention his plans for the next day to Jack, Mabel would suggest something for Sally to prepare for meals. Jack enquired after Peter and was told that he was at high school in Adelaide. This brought a direct look to Sally, whose head was down as usual. But no comment was made. Most of the conversation came from Charlie who was forever the chatter box.

After about a week, Sally assumed that Jack was already out in the paddocks with her father, and no longer hoped to see him in the morning. She had forgotten about Sunday. On Sundays the men did not work. The women and girls still had to of course, because meals still had to be prepared and cows milked etc.

'Hello' he said. 'I see you now have a pony. Will she still let you ride her? You have grown awfully tall.' In fact, Sally had not only grown tall, but beautiful. She had long wavey auburn hair, pale faultless skin and a figure which any twenty five year old woman would be proud of.

'Her name is Dolly. And I am the *only* one she will let ride her. I might be tall, but I am not particularly heavy.' This with quite a scornful attitude. 'She is a very strong horse and would probably let me ride her even if I weighed as much as you.' At this last comment Sally blushed. She didn't mean to imply that Jack was heavy. She didn't really know what she meant. She was surprised to see him there.

'Well, p'raps we'll see one day if Dolly will let me ride her.' Jack responded. Sally grinned at that comment. She knew the pony would not let anyone but her ride it. Still, she didn't want to discourage Jack. He did have a confident air about him and it would do him good to come off a pony. Though she was pretty sure he could hold his saddle on a full size horse.

Jack took something out of his pocket and let the pony smell it, then eat it. He gently reached behind the animal's ear and gave it a good scratch. Dolly gave a gentle snort and nuzzled into Jack's shoulder.

'Traitor' said Sally.

'Who? Me or your pony?' asked Jack, and he sauntered out of the stable and left Sally to her milking. It was at this point, if Sally had been a few years older, she would have said "Men!" in that universal way that women sometimes do.

The harvest season was starting soon. This year David was determined to make a profit, so he had engaged two more young men to help. They all bunked together in the room in the big shed. A bunk bed was added to accommodate them all. They all ate their meals with the family. These meals were now taken in the dining room. Having three extra blokes in the kitchen was just too much for Mable and Sally. Preparing meals kept Sally and her mother very busy. And for once they were able to make use of all the milk Daisy provided. Every four days they would walk to their nearest neighbour, laden with milk, and borrow the use of their separator to make cream. It was a laborious process, but similar in a strange way to putting the wash through the clothes wringer. There was a lot of hand cranking involved. Still, the cream was worth it. They were now able to make butter. They had bought a butter churn themselves, from Mabel's music money, but they could not stretch to a cream separator. Besides, the churn was a small contraption compared to the separating machine. Back at the farmhouse, the cream, milk and butter, plus any other perishables were kept in a Coolgardie safe. The flow of air over wet hessian sides kept contents cool. There was no need for an ice box on the farm. Besides, there was no icemaker in the town yet.

So, while the men were labouring out in the paddocks, the women were labouring in the kitchen and laundry. All of this left very little time for flirting with one particular farmhand. But he was a resourceful chap that Jack. Most mornings Sally would be disturbed in her milking by Dolly's gentle snorting and she knew that Jack was approaching. He used the excuse of feeding the pony so that he could get in a few words with the girl. No-one was the wiser. The other two workers stayed in bed for as long as they could. The animals in the stable were Sally's responsibility, so she knew none of her family would appear. It was a very good arrangement. Over time a strong friendship developed between the two. The thirteen years age difference simply did not exist in their minds. Sally really was quite mature for her age, and Jack took great care not to cross any boundaries. There was something about this girl that made his heart swell. If he accidentally got too close to her, he noticed that other parts of his anatomy swelled as well. She was just a child, so he was extra careful not to let this happen too often.

One day, when they had settled into their quiet conversation over the milk bucket, Sally asked him.

'How come you're not married with a couple of kids? Most blokes your age are. Even young Ginger who helped with last year's harvest was married. He had a wife in Port Lincoln who was expecting her first baby.'

'I came close once.' Replied Jack. He turned to look directly into her eyes. A solemn look came over his face. Sally had not seen this expression on Jack before and she suddenly wished she hadn't asked the question. 'There was a girl in Port Lincoln I knew when I was working on the cray boats there. We even got engaged. But before the wedding I just knew it wasn't right. I mean, I liked her 'n all, but I found it hard to have a decent conversation with her. She was full of "when we get married this and when we get married that". I think in the end she would have married anyone who would take her away from her folks. That's not what I want. I want to marry someone who wants to share her life with me because she loves me. I want to share my life with her because I love her. There has to be a bond between us that nothing will break.'

Sally had not expected such honesty from this man. Men didn't usually talk about feelings and love and such stuff. His whole reply was like it was from a romance novel she had secretly read a couple of years ago. It was strange, her emotions went from jealousy when he confessed to being engaged once, to wonderment as he talked about what he wanted from such a commitment as marriage.

Sally looked him square in the face. 'How can you forge a bond with someone when you travel all over the country so much?'

His brown eyes seemed to reach right inside of her. 'Well, let's just see how we go shall we?'

And with that he walked away.

CHAPTER 5

Harvest 1937-1938

It looked like being the best harvest yet. With three helpers, David was confident they could bring it all in. Even the jute grain sacks were cheaper this year. Mind you, when they were picked up from the local stock and station agent they had a nest of mice in them. Quickly dealt with though. The wireless said that Australia was nearly through The Great Depression. Things were looking up. Not that this necessarily related directly to the farmers in this area. The government did have various schemes on offer throughout 1929 to 1935. However, these schemes were hard to navigate, difficult to apply for and simply didn't seem to understand what a farming family might need by way of assistance. The one good help the government gave was its partial support of the farmworkers.

Running a farm was so labour intensive that unless a chap had a swag of sons, it was well neigh impossible to get through the seeding and harvest process. David managed the seeding on his own, but it was a long haul. The seed was traditionally planted in autumn, just after the break in season. If the rains came late, David couldn't start. And if they came early he had to hope there was not too much rain which would cause the old plough to bog. The horses were reliable, but the weather was not.

He was never quite able to seed all the land he wanted to in a season. Mostly though, he got a lot of it done. One of the government assistance schemes was to subsidise the cost of fertilizer. What the government didn't seem to understand was that if there was no money to buy fertilizer at all, there was nothing to subsidize. So if anything did get that little bit of extra help from superphosphate, it was the flattest, most easily accessed areas of the farm. Sadly, this was also the areas which would get waterlogged if there was too much rain.

It seemed like the stars were all aligned for the coming harvest. David had noticed an increase in the mice population, but he wasn't concerned by it.

Farm life was running reasonably smoothly. David was happy with his workers. He had a particular liking for Jack who had worked for him before. The other two workers were a bit lazy, a bit disrespectful and a bit ignorant. But, he took what labourers he could get, and used Jack as a kind of supervisor.

Jack and Sally had their morning tate-a-tate every day and were forming a strong friendship in their limited conversations.

Mabel and Sally spent a lot of time cooking and tending to the garden. The house tank was full of water so the plants got as much water as they needed. Daisy got extra feed and very kindly produced extra milk. Cream was made on a more regular basis and most of it turned into butter. There was always enough cream left for the smoko scones for the workers. The whey was used in the daily bread making process. Nothing was wasted or thrown out. The farming families had got through the worst of the great depression simply because they grew a lot of their own food. Clothes were hand made, handed down, handed around, altered and eventually turned into cleaning rags. Old jumpers were unpicked and knitted into something else. Food scraps went to the chooks. Even the mice caught in the mouse trap in the larder were thrown to the chooks for extra protein. Fallen leaves and twigs were saved for the stove and sitting room fire in winter. Fallen logs of course, were chopped to feed that ever hungry wood stove in the kitchen. The family themselves didn't need much, but the farm did. Any money brought in from harvest or the small amount of wool from shearing was spent on the farm. It was Mabel's music money which bought flour and other staples. Shoes for the growing Charlie were needed every year. She and Sally shared their footwear being the same size by the time Sally was twelve. New dresses were a rarity and mostly came as gifts from either David's sisters or Mabel's sisters back in Adelaide. Mabel managed to pay for tennis memberships for the entire family and allowed Sally to continue with her golf. The girl really was very good at sport.

Only Charlie went back to Adelaide over Christmas that year. David went with him to catch up with Peter and see how his schooling was progressing. He planned to be away only about five days. During David's short absence, Jack was in charge of the other workers and the harvest was to continue. This was a much shorter stint in Adelaide than was normal for David. Charlie was to stay the entire six weeks of the school holidays and then be sent home on the train in the company of another local family. Sally, again felt like she didn't have a say in things. Surely her mother could manage on her own for a few days. She wanted to see Peter. But more importantly, she wanted to see her friend Josie. She had so much to share with her about Jack. And for some reason, she wanted to talk to Josie's mum. There were confusing things going on within her which she simply could not talk to her own mother about. As it was, David insisted that Sally stay at the farm.

Not surprisingly, there was a telegram sent to Mabel on the day David was expected back. He had been delayed and would be away another couple of days.

These frequent, and to Sally's mind, unnecessary absences from the farm by her father worried the girl. She didn't miss her father when he was away, quite the contrary. The house hold seemed to be generally more content when David was not there. There was less bickering from her parents. Her mother smiled more often. Charlie didn't stammer so much and she enjoyed a little more independence. Having more responsibility did not bother her at all. No. there was just something going on that Sally felt was important, but couldn't discuss it with anyone. But that December visit of her father's played on her mind. He was only supposed to be away for five nights and it suddenly extended into seven. No explanation given.

After the arrival of the telegram, she decided to ask Jack about it.

'Dad's going to be away a couple more days.' She said the next morning when she heard him approach the milking stand, then trample of couple of mice. 'I don't understand why he spends so much time in Adelaide. I'm sure it has nothing to do with the farm or checking on Peter or even visiting the aunts. I think there is more to it than that, but I don't know what.'

Jack could tell she was despondent. Should he tell her what he knew? She was only fourteen, but what he knew might eventually effect the whole family. He did not want to lie to this girl. He would never lie to her. He had every intention of this girl being in his life forever. He just couldn't tell her that yet.

'He's got a woman in Adelaide.' Jack said quietly and tenderly. He expected an eruption but what he got was the saddest look he had ever seen on such a lovely face.

'How do you know?' she asked.

'Word travels all over this area. Your dad can be a bit loose with his tongue when he's had a drink. Some bloke at the pub had heard it from some bloke who heard it from some other chap and so on. No one ever tells any women, but one of our lads here heard it and passed it on to me. I'm sorry Sally, but it's been going on for years.'

'What should I do?' She was beginning to get angry now.

'Nothing. Absolutely nothing. You cannot interfere in your parent's life. Besides, if he had even an inkling that you knew, it would come back on one of us workers, likely me. Cause who else do you speak to but ladies at the tennis club. And they sure don't know.' He reached out to touch her face. 'You can talk to me about anything Sal, but you must never let your mum know, or confront your father. I'm sorry sweetheart, but it's for them to sort out, not you.'

He had never called her sweetheart before. He had never touched her face before. Suddenly, she wanted to fall into his arms. She wanted to feel his strength around her. She wanted to feel his surety around her, like he would always look after her. But she didn't move from the milking stool. Her mind was in turmoil and her pulse was racing. But she didn't move her position on the stool. She was only fourteen and he was twenty seven. No one would ever understand. No one would ever approve. She felt even more alone than she had before this conversation. A mixture of shame and anger welled up inside her. She felt betrayed by her father and shame at his behaviour. And every bloke in the district knew what was going on.

She finished with the cow and left the shed not saying another word to Jack. Jack went back to his bunk room and got ready for the day's work.

Time passed, as it always does. Sally turned fifteen. The harvest was finished and it did indeed look like a good one. All the bags were ready to be loaded onto the cart to take in to the holding sheds in town. In fact this year they reckoned that there would be two trips into town. This season a harvest dance had been arranged in Minnipa. Mabel's dance band would be playing of course and David thought it a good idea that all the workers as well as Sally attend. Charlie was still in Adelaide and he didn't really want Sally left alone on the farm.

The old Bedford truck was loaded up with wife, daughter and on the tray the three farmhands.

In the week before, much fussing with pins and ribbons had been going on in the farmhouse in an attempt to make an old dress of Mabel's look like a new dress for Sally. The men folk had to make do with clean shirts and mended trousers. No-one complained. It was the first such celebration in the district for a long time. Sally's usual calm demeanour deserted her to the point where her mother had to tell her to stop "prattling on" so much.

'Sally, when you are at the dance you must dance with everyone who asks you.' Mabel said as she gathered up her music sheets. 'It would not be polite to just dance with one person all night.'

Sally blushed. Did her mother know what was going on in the cow shed?

'I don't really expect anyone to ask me to dance Mum. Unless it's Dad just being polite.'

Mabel gave Sally a look that only mothers can. Mothers all over the world know when their daughter is infatuated with someone. They may not know who the focus of that infatuation is, but they know what their daughter is going through.

'I'm sure you will have a lovely time dear. Just try to remember how old you are because in that dress, you look eighteen, not like a girl who is only fifteen.' Mabel continued with her preparations to leave.

Sally thought that this was about the closest she and her mother had ever been. The time they spent getting the dress ready. Sally had listened to her mother's piano rehearsals for the dance music. New sheet music had been posted in from Adelaide but the band had to practice as individuals because there was not the chance to get together. Sally pretended to be the violinist and that made her mother smile. She liked seeing her mother smile. She secretly knew that was why she pretended to play the violin rather than pretend to be playing the saxophone like Mr Walker from the general store.

The short trip into town was uneventful. Although, there was a bit of cleaning up of seats beforehand because a family of mice had chosen the straw stuffing as their breeding nest. David frowned at the mice. They were becoming a bit too prevalent for his liking. He wondered if anyone else was having the same trouble. He would find out tonight anyway, as every farmer in the district would be at the harvest dance. And if they weren't there, they would be at the pub, which is exactly where he intended to spend most of the evening.

It was a wonderful night. The Church Hall had been decorated with flowers from people's gardens. There were flowering manna gum branches hanging from the rafters with bailing twine. A long refreshment table had been set up with huge glass punch bowls and tiny glasses. Sandwiches and cakes galore.

The family arrived early to allow for the band to have a quick rehearsal of the newest and latest tunes. The men went to the pub for a quick one and Sally stayed at the hall to help some of the local women set up the supper table. Her eyes flitted to the stage every few minutes during the practice runs of the music. Was she the only person who saw how close Reg stood to her mother? How they seemed to have some hidden communication about the music. About other things. Since her conversation with Jack about David's infidelity she seemed to see adults flirting with other people's partners everywhere. Even Mr Walker seemed to take a particular interest in Mrs Beasley from the Post Office. She had brought along a tray of lamingtons for supper and Mr Walker practically jumped off the stage to help her carry them. If this is the way grown ups behave, she thought, I don't particularly want to get any older than fifteen.

Sally did dance with every man who asked her. Which meant she danced every dance. Jack was careful not to monopolise her. Her asked her for every third dance. My goodness that man knew how to dance. The first time he held her in his arms she had never felt so safe in her life. He directed her around the dance floor with the ease of a professional ballroom dancer. And she, a girl who had only danced in the kitchen before, to the music on the wireless. It did seem like most of the other farmhands in the district had the same lessons. Just jiggling along and tripping over their own feet. But some of the local boys had been taught by their mothers. It turned out that Sally was a natural dancer. Just like she was a natural on the tennis court or golf course. David didn't ask his daughter to dance. He was at the pub. It was probably just as well, because she knew people were watching her closely every time she danced with Jack. Well, it seemed that way to her. She kept saying over and over in her mind 'fifteen and twenty eight. fifteen and twenty eight.' It was the only way she stopped herself from falling into his arms and never leaving them.

When the last dance had finished and the band was packing up, Jack wandered over to the pub to retrieve David. He deposited him in the back of the truck declaring his boss too drunk to drive. There were more people wanting rides home than rides available due to inebriated drivers, so Mabel insisted that she could get a ride back with Reg. Jack bundled a few extra bodies into the old Bedford and acted as taxi driver. It took them an extra hour to get home. Surprisingly, Mabel was not there yet.

'A bit of trouble with the car.' Reg said when he eventually dropped Mabel off. David was already asleep. But Sally wasn't. She was waiting up for her mother to get home.

'Suspicion confirmed' she thought to herself.

No-one commented at breakfast.

The next day it rained. And rained and rained. February was far too early for a break in the season. Summer was still officially having its time. There was a mad rush to cover the bags of wheat. Not enough tarps.

'Move them in to the shed' David ordered. Daisy and Dolly were turfed out of their stalls. The work horses were confined to the stable yard behind the shed. No sheltering for them tonight. The men worked frantically in the pouring rain to get the grain under cover. The bags had been stacked up in the lee of the stables waiting for word to come from the storage sheds in town to bring in the grain. On his previous night's sojourn at the pub, David learnt that none of the farmers had been told to bring in their loads yet. 'A bit of a problem in the sheds' they said. It turned out, according to the local stock agent, that the problem was mice. 'The railway sheds were full of the little blighters. The bosses at The Port had even sent

out some "exterminators" to deal with the problem.'
Apparently, the floor was not yet clear enough to allow
the grain to come in.

The next morning, the damage became glaringly
obvious. There were trails of grain everywhere. Nearly
all the bags of grain had holes in them. Holes meant
there might be mice inside the bags. Not only that,
the bottom row of the bags were damp. The jute held
up pretty well to rain, but when the barrier had been
breached, as in eaten, the grain started to spoil.

The harvest being officially over, two of the farm
workers had contracts elsewhere in the state. Jack had
been engaged to stay a few weeks longer to help David
service equipment and do whatever could be done to
prepare for seeding. Now, he was needed to re-bag
the grain. Together he and David emptied each bag
of wheat and oats. Additional bags and binding had
to be brought in, and of course this was in very short
supply. Every farmer in the district was in the same
predicament. Wives and children were called on to
help. School was late starting which fortunately freed
up Charlie, who had just returned from Adelaide. All
the school children from farming families, even those
not from farming families, helped out their friends
where they could.

The grain was laid out on the threshing table. Then the workers, of all ages, had to go through, by hand, and retrieve any wet grain, mouse droppings and dispense with any pups. Adult mice scampered everywhere. This of course caused another problem because if they were left alive, they would breed. Those farmers who had dogs had extra help in this hunt. David's family did not. It was boring, back breaking work.

Meanwhile, Daisy still had to be milked every morning. She was not happy being relegated to a holding yard and lean to. It was also difficult for Sally to confine the animal to keep from being kicked. The cow wouldn't mean it of course, but it could and did happen. In the end, Jack would come and lean against the broad flank of the cow while Sally milked. Their illicit, unspoken (even to each other), romance, was blooming. In public, the rules still applied. She did not speak to the farmhand unless it was absolutely necessary. But she did look at him, and he at her. How on earth did they think that no-one would notice that those looks were not just "work related"?

It was David who caught them. Sally had just drained the last of the milk from Daisy's fourth quarter and was turning to rise from the milking stool. Jack bent down and gently put his arm around her to help her up. They were so close. Their clothes touching. It was inevitable. Jack kissed her gently on the lips. Softly, tenderly. Nothing urgent or even sexual. It was a kiss of chaste love. And it was Sally's first kiss. But all David could see as he strode around the corner of the shed was Jack with his lips on his daughter.

'Eileen Meredith Chandler!' He shouted. Using her full and proper name. 'Get up to the house this minute.' He was bellowing. Anger screamed from his mouth. 'And you, you bloody bastard, pack your things and get out.' This to Jack.

There was no arguing of course. The boss, the girl's father had said his piece and there was to be no discussion. Jack needed to tell Sally that he would not leave the district, but there was no way to get a message to her. She was confined to the house until David was sure the "bastard" had left the property. He never called his daughter "Sally" again.

CHAPTER 6

1938

The re-bagging of the grain continued in stoney silence for the next week or so. In the end, David calculated he got about half the gain he originally had into the storage shed at the rail terminal. Most of the farmers in the area had about the same proportion. Which of itself, would have meant a fairly good return for the season. Problem was, that as well as being a bumper crop in their area, albiet mouse plagued, every region in the state also had a bumper crop, with no mouse problems. The price of grain plummeted with the oversupply. In all, that year's harvest returned the farm about the same money as a very poor year. Another very poor year for the books.

Sally was miserable. She missed Jack so much. He had become her best friend. She also suspected that she was very much in love with him. How could this have happened to her, she wondered. She had put all her defences in place against her heart, but to no avail. She knew from that kiss that Jack was not going to take advantage of her. She knew that he loved her. She, a girl of fifteen, with very little experience of the world outside her farming community. Was it even possible for a man of twenty eight to fall in love with a fifteen year old girl? All of this was a waste of time anyway. He was gone. She knew for certain that her father would never let him back on the property. She hated her father and was disappointed in her mother. Charlie was only ten years old and a very strange boy. Peter, her only hope in this family, was having a wonderful time at high school in Adelaide and was no help or comfort to her at all. She felt so alone.

Things had quietened down on the farm. It would be a couple of months at least before seeding started. School, for those attending, had resumed. With the frenzy of harvest, Sally had not ridden her pony for some time. She decided to rectify that and rode out to visit old Willy-Jack. who still remained on the property.

She dismounted and stood quietly, with Dolly gently nuzzling her neck, outside the rickety whirly waiting for the old Elder to appear.

'He leaving soon.' The old man said as he eventually took up his squatting position near his cold camp fire.

'Oh' said Sally. 'He has already left. My father kicked him off the farm two weeks ago.'

'Not the smoking bloke. He will never leave you Missy' said Willy-Jack as he drew circles in the dirt with a stick. Sally noticed the circles intertwined. 'I mean the boss man. He leaving soon. Not coming back.'

Sally was very perplexed. She lead her pony back to the house, not having the inclination to ride after that little bit of "wisdom" from the old man. Surely her father would not walk off the farm and leave his family to fend for themselves. She knew he had a mistress in Adelaide, but men did not leave their wives and children. It simply was not done. And what was that bit about Jack never leaving her. He was gone. That was that.

Two weeks later David made a trip to Adelaide. 'To see if his sisters would extend him a loan. He said.

He did not come back.

After three weeks and no word, Sally and her mother realized David would not be back. There proceeded a flurry of letters from Mabel to David's sisters enquiring of his whereabouts. The sisters replied, but David did not. The sisters said they were not prepared to lend or gift him anymore money. If the farm could not support itself, they could not afford to lose even more money on the venture. As to David's whereabouts, they could not say.

'Would not say.' said Sally after reading the letter aloud, for the second time. She did not mean to be disrespectful to her aunts, even though they were hundreds of miles away, but she was angry. Angry that her father had left them. Angry at her father's lack of farming skills or knowhow. Angry at nature for turning a bumper harvest into a failure. Angry at her father for getting rid of Jack. And, to be honest, angry at Jack for leaving her. With all that, she was not too fond of her mother either for pretending her little secrets.

'You know he's got a woman in Adelaide.' She blurted out to Mabel. They were washing the dinner dishes, Charlie had already gone to bed. The plate in Sally's hand crashed on the floor. It was hard to pretend it was an accidental drop, not a deliberate smash.

'I know.' said Mabel, as she bent to pick up the pieces of crockery.

'You know! How long have your known?'

'I've always known, Sally. And before this one there were others. Fidelity was never high on your father's priorities.'

'And your fidelity Mum?' she said quietly. Her voice was faltering and tears had started to fall.

'Never mind about me Miss. What do you think you were doing with that man who is twice your age?' Mabel was getting angry herself now. Not because her daughter had accused her of something, but because the whole situation was becoming overwhelming for her.

'He was twice my age when I was thirteen. Now he's not. And every year it gets less.' Sally had already worked out the maths in case this argument came up.

'And all I did was kiss him Mum, I promise.' The tears were streaming by now. Both women were emotionally exhausted. Yes, in Mabel's eyes, Sally had suddenly become a woman. And what a mess she had landed in to commence her womanhood.

Mabel gently took her daughter's hand and sat her down. She reached up and took down two sherry glasses from the sideboard. The sherry was kept openly on the top shelf of the cabinet. A little sherry while preparing dinner was often welcomed.

'If we are going to get through this Sally, we are going to have to work together. No more arguing.' Mabel passed a small glass of sherry to her daughter. 'I will need you to ride into town tomorrow and make some phone calls from the post office. In the mean time, I want you to think about what Willy-Jack said to you. I don't particularly put much store in the old native, but he was right about Jack coming back after all those years. He was right about your dad leaving. Maybe he is right about Jack hanging around.' She dabbed at her daughter's tears with her own hanky. 'Perhaps you could ask if he has been seen at the stock and station agent. Say your Dad is looking for him. No need to let the town know about our personal problems just yet.'

The next morning, after slipping Charlie off the rear of her pony at the school, Sally proceeded into town to the post office. She posted the letter her mother had written the night before. It was addressed to the Land Department. No doubt her mother was letting them know that the annual lease money was not available this year. Sally knew it was unlikely to be available again, but she doubted her mother would confide that just yet. Then she asked to use the public telephone and gave the post mistress the number for her aunts in Adelaide. Surprisingly, Mrs Beasley gave Sally complete privacy for her phone call.

'Hello Aunty G' she said cheerfully when the phone was answered. 'Would you please give me the phone number for Dad's friend Kathleen Eggleston.'

Complete silence at the other end of the line. A long pause. Sally could imagine the turmoil her aunt was in. *"How does she know that name? Does she know? She must know. Well, his family has got to find out eventually. I will no longer protect him even though he is my little brother. It is not right what he has done."* All this thinking from all the way over in Adelaide.

'Yes dear. Just a minute. Do you have a piece of paper? Good. The number is 752 on the Burswood exchange. Are you managing alright Sally? How is your mother and little Charlie?' Aunty G had spent so long in shock that Sally's three minutes was nearly up.

'We are all doing splendidly thank you Aunty. Give my love Aunty E'. Cheerful lies over the telephone. Sally hung up before the conversation could continue.

Having got the telephone number for her father's "other woman" Sally now didn't have the confidence to carry out the next step of the plan she and her mother had made up. I need to do this. I need to find out what will happen to us. Better get on with it she thought. She asked Mrs Beasley to connect to the new number. Terribly professional Mrs Beasley didn't make a sound. Just dialled the relevant numbers on the post office telephone. Ring ring, Ring ring.

'Burswood 752. Kathleen speaking'. Mature, polished voice. About the same age as her mum, Sally thought.

'May I speak to my father please?' Ever so polite. Sally stood up straight and assumed her most mature voice. No reply. Long pause. Here goes another 3 minutes of wasted silence thought Sally.

Eventually, her father's voice.

'How did you get this number?' David wasn't really angry, but he was surprised to hear from his daughter, not his wife.

'Dad we know you are not coming home, but we need to know what will happen to the farm.' Sally completely ignored his question. The answer was obvious and she was not inclined to make small talk.

'I'll write to your mother.' David responded rather abruptly. Clearly he was not in the mood for small talk either.

'Very well then. If we haven't heard anything within two weeks I'll call again.' Sally and her mother had gone through all sorts of scenarios and so far this was following scenario three exactly. She disconnected the line.

Suddenly, the enormity of these telephone calls was too much for her. Sally wilted against the post office wall. Her hands were shaking and her eyes were clouded up with tears. She felt so weak.

Mrs Beasley, professional or not, had heard every word and was rather quick in supplying a chair and a glass of water for Sally. However, she made no comment, thank goodness, offered no sympathetic words or gestures. After a little while Sally regained her composure. She nodded sagely to Mrs Beasley and left the post office and headed for the stock and station agent.

It turned out that the farmhand called Jack had been into the store a few days ago. He was picking up some supplies for Bill Morrison. Bill was a farmer about five miles out of town on the opposite side to Sally's farm. (Was it her farm now?) One vague message was left. Should he be seen again, that her father, David Chandler, was wanting to catch up with him some time. All very casual and non committal. Sally hoped that the local gossip did not move too quickly and Mrs. Beasley remained silent. And even if the gossip mill already had it out there that David was gone, the intent of the message to Jack would be understood.

Sally cantered all the way home and related everything to her mother. That evening, another glass of sherry was shared.

Jack turned up three days later.

It took several months, many letters and an occasional telephone call, but by the end of the year Sally, her mother and Charlie had packed up their personal belongings and taken a train to Adelaide. During those months, Jack was an occasional visitor to the farm and offered what help he could with liaising with the Land Department, other farmers, and David's creditors (of which there were many). There was no money left in the bank and Reg had helped with train fares and a few other small things. No one wanted him to be seen as helping Mabel out. For as long as she could Mabel continued with her music teaching and performing. Jack continued working for Bill Morrison. He even played golf with Bill. He tried to stay away from Sally and her mother as much as possible. He did not want to bring more shame on them. They exchanged messages and furtive smiles at the golf club, at Church and at the stock and station agent. The farm was eventually reallocated to one of the local farmers with a neighbouring property. David's family did not own the land, and therefore not the house. There was only the livestock and implements to be sold. The farming life was over for this family. Charlie had just turned eleven, Sally was sixteen, and Peter was fourteen and still being supported by one of Mabel's sisters. Mabel was officially a "deserted wife".

What would become of them?

CHAPTER 7

1939-1945

Sally was invited by Josie Wright's family to live with them in Eden Hills. With her mother's permission she readily accepted. In this family she felt loved and accepted. Josie was a very good friend and her parents were no-nonsense people but generous with their parental guidance and love. Something Sally felt she lacked from her own mother and father. She did not expect these kind people to support her financially. They had two children of their own although both Josie and her older brother were working. Sally found employment at a pharmacy in the area. Occasionally she would take the train into Adelaide and help out at the pharmacy her great grandfather had started. This was easily achieved because at that time her Aunts Ethewin and Gertrude also did some hours there. Sally did not harbour any ideas of becoming a chemist like her great grandfather, but she was proud to work as a shop assistant at Birks' Chemist in Rundle Street. The pharmacy in Eden Hills however, where she spent most of her working time, was very convenient to the Wright's home where she lived.

Mabel and Charlie stayed with Mabel's mother and Peter continued with the education his maternal aunt was providing. He was now boarding at an agriculture college and enjoying it very much. Sally was still jealous of her brother's education opportunities, but not of her brother personally. David was openly living with Kathleen. She had not been married previously and had no children of her own. It was incredibly scandalous in those days for this domestic situation to occur, so to ease life for everyone, Kathleen called herself Mrs Chandler when they took up residence together. The real Mrs Chandler, Sally's mother, eventually rented a house with Reginald and young Charlie lived with them. Mabel became known as Mrs Brown. Although spread out over the city of Adelaide, they none the less still functioned as a family, although it was very difficult at times.

Contact was at last made with David, but there was not a lot of interest or enthusiasm on either side.

It was all very disturbing to Sally. Whenever she was reminded of the situation her head went down and a frown appeared on her face. She did not smile very much. Her parents and their new partners seemed to cope with it all quite well. But Sally felt embarrassed and ashamed. She never talked about her parent's domestic situations with anyone. She truly appreciated the Wright family for their love and caring. But she missed the easy conversations she had with Jack.

In September of 1939 war was declared by Britain against Germany and Australia chose to join the war effort.

"Dear Sally,

So glad to hear that you are happy living with the Wrights. It must be really strange knowing that your father and Kathleen are living together. Does she call herself Mrs Chandler to satisfy the neighbours? And how does your mum handle it? Though, Reg is a good sort and I am sure they will find a way to work things out.

Sal, you know that there is fighting going on over-seas and it might come here. Well, not if I can help prevent it. I know I am only one bloke, but there are plenty of blokes signing up to join the forces. I want to join the Airforce. What do you think?

Love from Jack"

Sally's immediate concern was for Jack. He was a fit young man of fighting age. Would she lose him, never having even got to know him properly? They continued their romance via letter. Jack declared that he would join the Royal Australian Air Force. He no doubt fancied himself a pilot, but of course, his lack of education was against him from the start. Still, he was determined to do his bit whatever it might be. Sally's friend Josie, who was a couple of years older than her, was training to be a nurse. This sounded like a worthwhile profession for a young woman, so Sally made enquiries as to how she could train as a nurse with the Airforce.

"Dear Jack,

I am so glad we are writing to each other. You were such a help to mum and Charlie and me when things went bad back home. I probably shouldn't call it "home" any more should I? Anyway, thank you.

I know you will want to do your bit in this war effort. Everyone does. If you think the Airforce is a good thing then go for it. But please Jack, stay safe.

I have decided to become a nurse, like Josie. I will be a couple of years behind her in training, but I think the Adelaide Hospital will take me when I turn seventeen which is not very far away. Josie stays at the hospital nurses' quarters as it is quite a big trip getting from here in the hills all the way across the city to the hospital. But she comes home when she has a few days off. I would do the same.

Please let me know where you end up Jack.

The whole parental situation is very strange indeed. I am so embarrassed. I don't talk to anyone about it. Mrs Wright says things just are as they are. There is nothing I can do about it. But I beg her not to tell anyone at Church or anything.

Love from Sally"

There was one fleeting visit from Jack on his way through Adelaide before travelling to Victoria for his training. Sally met him at the train station in Adelaide. They only had a couple of hours together, but it was more than either of them had hoped for. They strolled down King William Street hand in hand. Sally, still quite shy was very self conscious, but Jack just beamed to have this beautiful girl beside him. They had tea at a café then walked back to the station to say their goodbyes. Each of them praying that it was not to be the last goodbye. Jack took Sally into his arms and kissed her. It was a much more grown up kiss this time. Sally simply melted. He had to hold her up till she found her feet again. With tears in her eyes she walked away from him. She could not bear to stand and wave goodbye from the platform like so many other young women and mothers were doing. She held on to her heart. She held on to her strength. She would not pine for this man she told herself. There is so much more in life that needed to be done. But her heart ached and her tears flowed.

This early in the war effort the Australia Defence Forces were not accepting women into their ranks. However, in 1941 the Royal Australian Air Force Nurses Service began and Sally joined up as soon as she could. She did her nurses training at the Royal Adelaide Hospital. Pretty soon, nurses were going to be in demand.

Meanwhile, Jack was undergoing training in Victoria. It was clear from his letters that he was never going to be a pilot. Or even a mechanic for that matter. Jack's skill set was limited to agriculture work and labouring. He was not alone in this. There were many reasonably intelligent young men who joined up who had never had the chance of a decent education as they were growing up. Jack was to train as a heavy machinery driver. Graders and such like were needed to build airstrips so that planes could land and take off. There were so many other "jobs" in the air force that Jack felt quite silly thinking that pilots were the only important ones. There were navigators, bombers and gunners, mechanics of course and his lot, the aerodrome staff.

The war was moving to the Pacific islands. The enemy there, and the greatest threat to Australian security, was Japan.

The letters continued.

"Dear Sally,

Well, I've finished my basic training. My unit is still based in Melbourne awaiting deployment. I'm not a pilot or anything exciting like that. They got me driving graders and other earth moving equipment as part of my training. I have the lofty title of "Grader Operator". Yes, I was taught how to use a gun and stuff like that. Do you remember the story I told you the first day I met you, about me riding my pony up and down the rows of an orchard and letting off shot to scare the birds away? You might not remember. You were such a shy little kid back then.

They say things are heating up in the Pacific with the Japanese having their eye on Australia. Gees, do they know how much desert we have here? And our cities are so spread out. Why would anyone want to invade Australia? Still, if that is the Jap's plan, then I will probably find myself building air-strips in some God forsaken island in the Pacific.

And yes, I will stay safe. I intend to come back for you Sally.

Love from Jack"

In 1942 a repatriation hospital was opened in Adelaide in the suburb of Daws Park. There were wounded soldiers coming back from the front in Europe and other places. As much as possible the powers that be wanted the men to recuperate in their home States. Sally had finished her training and was wearing the Royal Australian Air Force Nursing Service uniform when she wasn't wearing her nurses uniform. She was now posted to the Daws Park Repatriation hospital.

"Dear Jack,

Things are heating up here too. I'm now based at a new (well, it was previously an old farm, but some buildings are new) repatriation hospital in Daws Park.

It is much closer to the Wright's place, so I catch the train down the hill and then a bus. Mr Wright is often waiting for me at the station when I get home from my shift. I have no idea what my real father is doing!

I have a new stripe to add to my RAAFNS uniform. I don't think I am cleverer than the other girls. But I definitely don't giggle as much!

What do you mean you're coming back for me Jack? Are you proposing?

Love from Sally"

Australia's involvement became more urgent when the Japanese forces began to advance toward Australia. Jack was posted to Indonesia. His unit was working closely with American forces. They seemed to have an unending supply of bombers and other aircraft. The Aussies had an unending supply of good humour and hard work.

"Dear Sally,
Yes, if you'll have me.
Love from Jack"

In 1943 Sally turned twenty one.

"Dear Jack,
Of course I will. When is your next Leave?
Love from Sally"
PS. I have another stripe. I am now a Sargent!

They were married in Melbourne later that year. It had to be Melbourne as that was where Jack's unit operated from. He was able to get leave, but only for two weeks. Sally for her part, managed to swing some leave in return for additional training at the base in Wagga Wagga. She borrowed a pretty day dress from a friend and managed to get a bridal bouquet. Jack wore his dress uniform. There was no reception and no wedding cake. But this was not unusual for a war time wedding, and neither of them was terribly upset about it. After a short honeymoon Jack was sent back to his posting in Indonesia. And after a bit of supplementary training in Wagga Wagga, Sally went back to Adelaide.

As it turned out, 1943 was a very busy year. Not only did Jack and Sally marry, but also Mabel and Reg and David and Kathleen married. The divorce between David and Mabel had come through. Ridiculously, David would not grant Mable a divorce earlier on, even though he was living with Kathleen. Mable and Reg had to admit to their "adultery" in order for the divorce to be granted. Such going's on back in the 1940's in conservative old Adelaide!

Adelaide was a conservative city. Even in the early part of the following century it was referred to as "The city of Churches". But part of its conservatism was that everything was so very well planned. Colonel William Light started mapping out the plan of the city in 1837. It became part of the Federation of Australia in 1901, along with five other British Colonies. And prior to that, in 1894 women in South Australia gained the right to vote. One of the first precincts in the world. There were of course many hinderances to the development of the city in the early years. The Colony of South Australia was a "free Colony". It was not a penal colony. Therefore, labour was in short supply. The climate was arid. It was isolated from the other settlements in the young country. And of course, it's settlers had no idea how to treat and get along with the original owners of the land. As in the rest of the country, the British just thought they could come in and take over someone else's land and not even give them much respect for the tens of thousands of years that the indigenous people had lived there and managed that land. However, the resilience and strategic planning of the Europeans eventually led to the development of a major urban centre in South Australia. Two world wars impacted this tiny city greatly. At the time of our story, the Second World War, saw the usual lack of "Man" power, supplies, rationing and the advancement of "Women" power into the workforce. Everyone had a job, but what goods and services were available were expensive, so the cost of living was high. But the community spirit was also high.

Sally was now a married woman although still living with her adopted parents in Eden Hills. Every day she treated young men who had been injured in that terrible war. Every day she feared for her Jack. This was a constant cause of worry for her. She was treating men who were injured in action. Her man was posted to a war zone. The fear of Jack being hurt was ever present.

With ongoing training, in nutrition and invalid care, in what would much later become part of the Adelaide University, Sally was at last getting the education she felt she deserved, but at what cost? The letters were infrequent and often a couple of weeks old by the time they arrived. But arrive they did.

"My Darling Sally,

That rifle training I had has stood me in good stead! I am still in Indonesia, but I can't tell you where I am. The Americans are based here. It is their airstrips we are building. Anyway, the place is crawling with Japs. They say that the Americans, with our help mind you, have taken back a lot of the islands the Japs took over a couple of years ago. Well, there are definitely still some here. The Yanks must have been busy doing something else because yesterday shots were fired across the strip we were grading. One bullet pinged my dashboard. I jumped down from the grader on the side I thought was safest and started firing in the direction of the jungle. I can't tell you everything that happened, but I did lose a mate. I'm OK Sally, but some of the Japs are not. When the Yanks got back from whatever it was they were doing, they rounded up the rest of the enemy and thanked us grader drivers very much.

Anyway, the talk is that the war will be over by the end of the year.

Love from your loving husband, Jack"

The war did indeed end in the latter half of 1945. Jack made it back home alive and uninjured. In 1945 both Jack and Sally were discharged from the Defence Services and their married life commenced.

CHAPTER 8

1945-1950

The man could not be happier. He had married the girl he fell in love with when she was only fourteen years old. He had waited till she was twenty one and then made her his own. Not only that, he had survived the war. Like many ex servicemen, he rarely spoke of his war experiences. In later years when speaking to his children, he made it sound quite boring. He "drove front end loaders and graders and built airstrips." Was about all he would reveal. When Jack returned to civilian street he was very much an average Australian bloke of the times. He was thirty six years old and still did not have a real trade. He hated the thought of driving graders in civilian life, but at times resorted to that, as at least he knew what he was doing. But he had good humour and a good work ethic. He put his hand to anything to bring in a wage, and build a life with his wife.

And Sally, how did Sally feel, now that she was a married woman? There never really was any question that she would marry Jack. Everyone just assumed it would happen. Her parents still did not approve, but that didn't matter because she did not approve of their marriage partners either. It was just accepted amongst everyone she knew that she would live happily ever after with this man who had waited so long for her. He was thirty four when they married. But, as Sally had calculated many years ago, every year the thirteen years between them seemed less and less. Time to take charge, as best she could, and get on with the life of wife and mother.

The mother bit started the following year with the arrival of a snowy haired boy they called George. At the time they were living in a one bedroom shack in the Adelaide hills which they had bought. They also bought a little grocery shop which Sally ran while Jack did whatever labouring work he could find. As was the custom at the time, the baby was put in a pusher out the front of the shop while his mum managed things inside. He would be given a stick of celery to chew on. He was much admired and seemed to revel in the attention of all who passed. Baby number two arrived nearly two years later. Mothering became a bit more difficult. This little girl, Marie, suffered badly from eczema. There were many hospital visits and medical bills started piling up. George, having been used to being the centre of everyone's universe became stroppy and difficult. The Wright family were close by and became honorary grandparents to the children. But it was still difficult managing two year old tantrums, a little girl continuously wrapped in bandages and suffering severe rashes, and running a green grocery shop. Jack was not always there. He went wherever the work took him. His pipe smoke permeated the little shack, so even when he was not around to help, its scent reminded Sally of him continuously. In the midst of all this, Jack's aged, contrary, father came to live with them. Jack's little family was the least financial of all his sibling and half sibling, but none of them would have the old man. Sally believed it was their duty to take the old chap in. He was a difficult man and really only added to her woes. But young George delighted in the old man and George Senior was very taken with his grandson and name sake. The whole situation, however, was getting too much for Sally.

Help arrived one day in the form of a black and white border collie dog. He turned up at the shop and would not be moved on. George fell in love with the dog instantly, and the feeling appeared to be mutual. The tantrums stopped. Now he was a "big boy" with responsibilities of his own. He had his very own companion that didn't scream all the time like his little sister Marie. Marie was in awe of the dog who had a very calming effect on her. Even the cat seemed to accept Prince. Sally was relieved that the children were settling at last. When Jack came back from a working trip north of Adelaide he just smiled at the dog, took Sally into his arms, and the world was a wonderful place.

Prince, the dog, proved his devotion to the family when they were forced to move into the downstairs flat of the aunts' house at Eden Hills. Sally's two maiden aunts had divided the huge big house into three parts by this time. The front flat was rented out. The middle section where the aunts lived, and the downstairs flat which was normally occupied by family members who had nowhere else to go at the time. On this occasion Jack and Sally had sold their little one bedroom shack and were awaiting the completion of a new house further away. The aunts did not like animals. So Sally's cat was rehomed with some neighbours and Prince was rehomed to a family north of Adelaide. Within five days Prince turned up at the flat. This was even more remarkable because he had only ever visited that house before, not lived there. He was returned to his new home some forty miles away. This time it only took him three days to make the trip back. He had to cross the river, negotiate city traffic and find his way through the hills to the house where the family was staying. The aunts relented and let him stay. He was not allowed inside the house, but he was happy sleeping in a shed. He was back with his family and that was all that mattered. Prince stayed with the family for another nine years. Eventually dying a peaceful and natural death.

The new house was completed at last. Sally was so proud. She had designed the house herself. She would never get to be an architect, but that didn't stop her from designing. With the sale of the grocery shop, Sally became a stay at home mum. Not that she was particularly happy with the role. Still, there was a garden to attend to and children to care for. There always seemed to be a relative of some kind living near by, or at least an assessable distance. Sadly, Marie continued to suffer badly from eczema. George, on the other hand continued to explore his adventurous spirit. Prince looked after them all. But he couldn't protect them from an epidemic which was sweeping Australia at the time and Adelaide in particular.

One evening, after the children were in bed, Jack noticed that Sally was somewhat pale. She was usually a very healthy girl his Sal. Tall, straight, long auburn hair and blue eyes.

'It's just a bit of a flu' said Sally. But as the evening wore on her breathing became laboured. She was vomiting and complaining of a sore neck. Being the nurse of the family she knew what this could mean. Jack immediately ran down the street to ring for an ambulance. Neighbours were called in to care for the children. Prince was on high alert.

Sally was diagnosed with polio. Polio at the time was a frightening, highly contagious illness caused by a virus. It was, and still is an incurable illness. For some the illness lasted only a few weeks, but for others it caused paralysis and many died. Children were most susceptible, but fit healthy adults were not immune.

Sally spent a year and a half in hospital. Her children were not allowed to visit her. The risk of contamination was too great. And at the time, medical staff were of the opinion that families should just "get on with life". Jack visited as often as he could, given the distance from jobs he was picking up and where everyone was living. The Hospital for Infectious Diseases was central in Adelaide, but living arrangements and work for Jack were not. It was a devastating time for Sally. There was no real treatment for the virus so it was just the symptoms which were treated. Pain relief, physiotherapy, such as it was in those days, assistance with breathing. Flat on her back. Unable to care for her children. Unable to do anything at all really. And the constant thought that she may not survive. It was a whole year before the recuperation process started in hospital. But she did survive.

The children stayed with their adoptive grandparents and Jack boarded with the Eden Hills aunts so he could be closer to the children. In truth, George had a wonderful time. He was the centre of attention and even started kindergarten while staying in Eden Hills. He was a bit young, but being a precocious little fellow, was well up to the task of getting himself there and back from the Wright's place. Jack kept Sally up to date with the goings on of the children. She was concerned about young George having to get himself to kindergarten, he was barely even four years old. His routine was to walk down the hill towards the railway station, turn right at the bridge across the rail lines then turn right again and go up the road to the C of E Church. Wait there to be joined by a little girlfriend and they were to be picked up by a taxi and taken the rest of the way to Kindy. After Kindy the reverse would occur. Indeed, this seemed like a big task for a four year old. One morning the taxi did not come, so George walked back home where his no-nonsense Grandma told him to go back and the taxi would come. He retraced his steps and indeed, the taxi did come.

The story was meant to cheer up Sally, but it only increased her anxiety. She was fiercely defensive of her little ones, even if they were quite independent. Perhaps this was in fact her fear. That the children would not need her anymore.

Marie was doted on by the old couple who became known as Oma and Opa. Mrs Wright was very mindful of the fact that the children had their own natural grandparents, and didn't want to cause too much confusion. Prince became Marie's guardian while George was at kindergarten. Sally would never have let her mother look after the little ones for such a long period of time and Jack was more than happy with the choice of carers. He travelled to work each day via train and bus. He had managed to pick up a more permanent job and this allowed him to be able to visit Sally whenever the hospital agreed to it.

Eventually Sally was released from hospital. The only visible sign of her long stay was a paralysed left arm. She wore a leather sling.

'It's not permanent'. She was told. 'You will get the use of your arm back. But you must exercise it as much as you can.' There was a family to look after so exercise would not be an issue. In the early 1950s the most modern household appliance was an electric washing machine. And the family could not afford one. The copper and wringer were still waiting for her in their house when she returned. She used her left hand as much as possible rather than her right. However, Sally was no longer the champion sports women she once was. There were other issues that Sally had to deal with too. She was sad a lot, and became short tempered. Jack noticed other slight changes in his wife's personality. But, in the early 1950s, mental health was not talked about, let alone treated. Society just expected her to get on with life and not look back. But it seemed to Sally, that life was always a struggle.

CHAPTER 9

1950-1956

Jack was a dreamer. Sally was a realist. The dreamer loved his realist with undying devotion. The realist did the best she could under the circumstances.

'What's this?' Sally asked when Jack presented her with a wrapped box a few weeks after her homecoming.

'Open it and see.' He said with a grin like a kid who got chocolate at Christmas time. Dutifully, she unwrapped the plain brown paper and took the contents out of the cardboard box.

'It's a typewriter.' She stated. Expression unchanged. Expression then slowly showing a mix of confusion, disappointment and general perplexity.

'But I can't type.'

'You can learn. You can do anything you put your mind to my darling, and it will help exercise your arm.'

The grin had faded, only to be replaced with that look of love that he always had for her when he knew she was disappointed. He always knew her moods and he tried his best to support her and turn things around.

'It's very nice Jack, but what would I want to type?'

'Well, you could try writing a book. You read quite a bit don't you? And you like learning about things. Perhaps you could write a book and just let your imagination run wild.'

Sally sighed. It was true that she read a lot of books. But they were usually biographies on interesting people. Jack only read fiction stories. She had no time for fictitious stories. But a gift freely given should be freely accepted. This was one of her many beliefs. It was very rare that she was given a gift of such value. It was a new typewriter. Probably one of the few new things the family had ever had, except for shoes. She would accept Jack's gift in the spirit it was given. But she still had no time for fantasies.

'If you don't think you could make up a story,' Jack offered. 'Perhaps you could type up a list of all the extended family. I find it difficult to keep up with who is who, and I am sure the kids are just getting more confused with every "aunt" they meet.'

This was very true. There were many in the extended family. Both she and Jack had aunts and great aunts. Some married, but surprisingly, mostly never married. There were step mothers and half siblings (on Jack's side) and step aunts and cousins (on Sally's side). Jack had recently discovered a whole lot of cousins he hadn't previously known about. And then, when they brought in the Wright children, who were now producing, and no blood relation at all, but very important, well, it all got quite confusing.

'Thank you Dear.' She said with genuine warmth. 'Perhaps it will be good for my left arm. I will start practicing tomorrow.'

Subsequently, not only the family tree, as she knew it, but every other piece of correspondence was then typed. Pressing the keys, changing the ribbon, winding the paper, even returning the carriage was practiced with her left hand rather than her right.

The dreamer had presented his realist a machine that no-one else in their circle of friends and relations possessed. She mastered it, and together over time, they worked a little miracle.

In 1955 the first vaccine against the poliomyelitis virus became available.

Jack got a real job for the first time in his life. Well, he was a salesman, on commission, but with a retainer which managed, just, to support the family. The parent company was a Swedish manufacturer of dairy separating machines. Milk was poured into the bowl and the centrifugal force of the spinning separated out the cream from the milk. These machines were sold all over the world. Australia's agriculture industry was picking up and the economy generally improving. There was the need for a branch in South Australia. Alfa Laval were looking for men with a background in agriculture and a personality for what today would be called a "soft sell". Not pushy and not overeducated. Jack was very short of formal education, but was not unintelligent. He could hold a conversation with any class of person. He made friends easily and of course, had spent his youth on Eyre Peninsular mixing with farmers of all persuasion. The catch was of course, the family would have to move to Tumby Bay on the east coast of Eyre Peninsular.

They had only been in their new house for about three years. One and a half of which Sally had spent in hospital.

'It will be good for us' Jack said, trying to jolly her along. 'George will be starting big school next

February. It will be nice to raise the children in the country rather than the city.'

Sally agreed in principle to that. But it meant leaving her support group of friends and family behind, and she was not entirely confident that she could cope with that. There were a lot of bad memories of failed farmers on the West Coast. She was, however, familiar with every town from Port Augusta at the top of the gulf all the way round to Ceduna and pretty much every town through the middle. She had read that the rail service was much improved with the growth in population and there was still the boat service from Port Lincoln to Adelaide. Besides which, she really had no say in the matter. Jack had organised the job and the posting without consulting with his wife.

The job provided a panel van which the family packed up with their personal possessions plus Prince and set off. It was a two day trip from Adelaide to Tumby Bay. The four humans sitting across the bench seat, the toddler sitting on her mother's lap and the dog spread across the floor of the cab. Sally's gradually strengthening arm was still in a leather sling when not in use. The family stayed in a hotel in Pt August on the way. This was the first time any of them had stayed, or dined, at a hotel. Sally and Jack's honeymoon had been a rented cabin in the Dandenong Ranges near Melbourne. At Whyalla the sealed road finished, so the last fifty miles was on gravel road. Slow and uncomfortable.

'Where's the house?' asked Sally when they eventually arrived in Tumby Bay. 'I thought we were buying a new Housing Trust House'.

'We are' replied Jack, but it's not finished yet. The firm has organised a small farmhouse for us to rent in the mean time. Its on the other side of town, about two miles out.'

Sally had become quite adept at hiding her disappointment, but Jack could feel it, and on this occasion, shared the feeling of let down with this wife. The "Farmhouse" had two bedrooms (good) and a telephone connected (Jack needed it for his work). But there was no electricity, no running water and the toilet was out the back. Kerosene and methylated spirit lamps provided lighting. The rain water had to be hand pumped to a holding tank for the chip heater in the bathroom. The fridge. There was no fridge. They had brought the icebox with them, but there was no ice to be had. Sally made do with a Coolgardie Safe and a Water Bag hanging from a tree out the back. Fortunately, being near the coast, there was always a breeze to fulfil the evaporation process of these two uniquely West Australian inventions. The laundry, as expected, was part of the back veranda. A large fire under a copper tub full of water to wash cloths. Then into cement tubs for rinsing. Extra Blueo rinsing for whites. Then the washing had to go through the double roller, hand wound mangler to squeeze the water out and then hung on the clothesline which had to be propped higher for things to dry. And all of this with an arm still weakened by polio, but it was improving. The only thing Sally found familiar was the wood stove in the kitchen. Well, that is not entirely true. She told herself. I had all these "modern conveniences" when I was growing up on the farm in Minnipa. Every time she did a load of sheet washing she was reminded of the very first time she saw Jack. He really hadn't changed much. Even the pipe was the same.

CHAPTER 10

Tumby Bay, as told by George

When the family arrive in Tumby Bay, George is five years old and Marie around three. Two more children will be added to the family over the next five years. This is the way George saw life in Tumby Bay.

It was an adventure full time for us two children. Like most country kids we were largely unsupervised, except by Prince. The dog also acted as chief snake catcher, and property protector. There were trees to be climbed, mud to play in and farming activities to observe. Even Dad rose to the occasion of being back in the country. He slaughtered and dressed the occasional sheep which was shared amongst neighbours. He shot and skinned rabbits to add to the family diet. One summer he was a volunteer fighting grass fires which often broke out in the paddocks as a result of thunder storms. Mum and Marie and I stayed home in the house. Goodness knows what we would have done if the fire had spread to the dry stubble around our place. The hardest part for Dad was having to go round and shoot wounded and distressed farm stock afterwards. He possessed a rifle and knew how to use it effectively. A skill he later taught me when I was deemed old enough.

Mum refused to plant a garden as she was adamant we would not be at that house long enough. She was right of course. After about a year the new house in Tumby Bay proper was finished and we moved again. Well, it wasn't right in Tumby Bay, more like the last street on the outskirts of the town. This suited me very well as there was bush on one side of the road and at the end of the street. It was like a whole adventure playground for Marie and me. But the snakes had mum worried. She killed more than one death adder during our time at Tumby Bay.

Mum & Dad stained the wooden floors then purchased and placed a carpet piece in the lounge. Our first fridge was quickly acquired – it was second hand and kerosene fuelled. New lino was bought and covered the kitchen floor. The Formica kitchen table had four *chairs so when Billy came along a bench was built by Dad, under the kitchen window. As it had been at the old farmhouse, wood was the fuel for bathing, cooking & heating. The irons were either metho fuelled or two rotated being heated by the wood stove.*

I have a memory of Oma and Opa flying to Pt Lincoln to visit us the first Christmas in the old farm house. Dad bought a crayfish straight off a boat for our dinner. I think Oma and Opa visited every year. This was an important event in Mum's life. This couple were her "adoptive parents" and a source of strength for her. Just about every time they came there would be a debate as they washed and dried dishes. Mum's position was that glassware then cutlery were to be dried before crockery. Oma's belief was that dishes were dried in the order they came from being washed. Dad's and my belief was that Oma only had one duty and that was to make a "Rolly Polly Pudding in a Bag".

Early in 1952 I started school. I was an eager student but had refused to learn numbers and spelling until then as I was going to school to learn such things. I was quite stubborn on the matter even though I had been repeatedly told that Jonathon Wright, two months my senior, was quite learned before he started school, and specifically able to achieve X, Y & Z in these areas. I suspect I was a bit of a handful and quite independent. There were later stories about how I would stamp my foot and refuse to budge on certain matters.

Now getting to school was a great adventure and one that I was going to do by myself. I walked the four hundred metres down the drive and crossed the Lincoln Highway and waited for the school bus. I had a new leather bag with straps that fitted across my back. The bus pulled up and I climbed aboard. I did not know any of the other children who ranged from my age (five) to fifteen. Once disembarked at the Tumby Bay Area School I realised I did not know which building I was supposed to go to. I followed some of the big boys up the steps into their prefab porch and started to hang my bag up on a hook – or at least tried to. School was going to be good. One of the boys said 'This is not your room' and directed me diagonally across the quadrangle to an old building where there were other children starting school. I could not work out why many of them, especially boys bigger than me, were crying! In hindsight for many of them it was their first time away from home and mum, whereas I had been to kindergarten and lived with another family for many months. We had changed homes many times, *so the first day at school was not as much of a strange event as for most. However, what I learnt years later, was that for Mum it was quite a stressful day. Unbeknown to me my parents had followed me in the blue work van, to the bus stop and then onto school. They saw me disembark, go into the wrong room, emerge, and then trot across the assembly area into the correct room. At that stage Mum was able to relax a little although she kept an eye out for the return of the bus (at the end of a full school day, no part days in those times), and my walk down the dusty driveway.*

The school bus was an old truck on which had been mounted a wooden framed cabin probably made of Masonite. There was a single row of seating down each side and across the front below a window that allowed the driver to monitor student behaviour. Very occasionally, as there was only one more stop to go, to drop off twin boys my age, I was allowed to sit in front with the driver. There was a door in the middle of the back wall and occupants were to open the door once the bus came to a halt at each stop. The new passenger would climb the steps, shut the door and after a pause for the latest passenger to find a seat, the bus would move on. On one occasion no one opened the door for me to get on. I clung to the step rail, about a foot above the steps, till we came to the next stop. I was lucky not to have my head knocked off when the bus did stop. I am not sure if not opening the door was a student prank or forgetfulness by onboard students. I did try bashing on the door but with the noise of the truck and rough road, apparently I was not heard. I do not recall telling Mum and Dad of this event – then I was always reluctant to tell of events of mine that went wrong. I may have become over self-confident with the life I led.

The first summer Mum and Dad tried playing Saturday tennis with the Tumby Bay Tennis Club. I only recall one Saturday of endeavours and do not recall them ever again playing tennis. I suspect the problem was Mum's polio induced weakness of her arm. They did later join the golf club and, although playing with second hand clubs, were regular players on the scrape tees, marginal and dry fairways and stony low scrubbed roughs in home competitions. Marie and I were usually left at the club house, although by about age eight I often stayed home – and that is another story.

Dad was a regular attendee at furniture auctions – ostensibly to see, and be seen by either current clients or other farmers who he could later follow up and try for a sale. In truth he was partly there to purchase furniture the growing family needed. Dad did maintain the reason for his wearing his hat and smoking a pipe was that these were features people would recognise as his, and be better able to relate to him when it came to selling. He needed all the help he could get to make a sale.

Similarly, part of Dad's routine was to attend the local show with an Alfa Laval stand. I remember an occasion, and am sure there were others, when he would attend horse races, boat races and other like events. The event that I recall was the Tumby Bay Annual horse races. It must have been during a school holiday (or Saturday) as I was allowed to accompany him. He spent the day with his mate Charlie Page and another who I think was Jack Randle, Charlie's boss. Not many races were watched as their main activity was drinking brandy at the bar. Dad and his mates became quite inebriated and they started boasting about various things. Dad's boast that I vividly recall was that 'Sally makes excellent pickled onions. They could not be bettered.' This was said with immense pride and I recognised his immense love for Mum and how pleased he was to be married to her. Luckily the racecourse was not overly far from Tumby and to the north thus requiring only three left turns and a looping right into our drive. I think the others followed him so they could have some of these famous pickled onions. Not sure of Mum's reactions but it was typical of Dad to arrive home with unexpected visitors. Mum had to be tolerant of these events and always "made do" with some food.

An aspect of Dad's care of Mum was revealed early in our time in the new house. We became the proud owners of a brand-new front load washing machine. To highlight this occasion it needs to be known that this type of machine were very new. For those lucky enough to have moved from the copper, troughs and mangle, to an electric machine, the pathway was via a top loaded machine. The purchase was made as Mum was experiencing considerable pain and discomfort with the old style copper etc. Unfortunately, our new washing machine was prone to experience regular breakdowns, so it was just as well the old equipment had been kept "in case of emergencies"!

Our dietary requirements were further supplemented by fish caught by Mum and Dad at the Main Jetty. Tommy roughs were the main catch although trevally were an additional but rare delicacy. Marie and I would accompany them as fishing was an evening event, with Dad scaling and filleting the fish, if caught, on our return home. Occasionally Dad would be invited to boat fishing or net fishing by one of the locals. These were generally more productive and we – Mum, Dad, Marie and me, but not Billy – would live on a range of fish for the next few days.

Money was short and leftovers were a norm although frequently dressed up as "bubble & squeak" or "Dev-illed Meat". Mashed potatoes were usually extended by including pumpkin in the mix. The home garden was well tendered, usually by Mum, and provided a vast array of vegetables, especially broad beans which I was forced to eat "because they were good for you." I do not miss them. Meat was usually hogget, with the only beef being rolled skirt or corned beef. Breakfast was Vita Brits followed by toast with vegemite and jam. Lunch was generally a white bread sandwich. We kids were not partial to healthy brown bread. Billy basically lived on fritz and sauce sandwiches. Fresh bread with apricot jam and cream was a common desert, which I still like.

During this period Dad took on two extra jobs. The first was sewing up wheat bags. This was usually done on summer evenings with the family, or at least a kid or more accompanying him out to a paddock. While Dad would sew up the bags and move them to *a nearby pile, we would play around. Payment was by the bag. This lasted several years. Another job started later was doing the books/accounts for one of the local garages. I think that before he started on this, or it may have been while doing this Dad studied Book Keeping by correspondence. This work was done on a Saturday morning and occasionally on a week day morning and probably some evenings.*

Annually we would go blackberry picking in the hills not far from Tumby. More accurately Mum would go blackberrying, with Billy in a basinet, while Dad, Marie and I would go yabbying. We placed a piece of mutton on a string and dropped it into a river pond. Once the string started to move we gradually pulled up the string and with luck, or Dad's help, pulled the yabby off the meat and placed them in a bucket of water. In the second and subsequent years we took a small home-made net, usually made from an onion bag, and placed this under the rising yabby. This was more successful.

Mum would gather a couple of billy cans of black-berries and we would end up with two or three dozen yabbies to be eaten that night after placing the live catch in boiling water. The blackberries were either eaten with homemade ice-cream or turned into jam.

It was usual for Marie and I, on the return journey, to lean over the side of the Ute, that replaced the earlier van, and fly aeroplane propellers – a smallish piece of dry bark placed centrally on a stick. That was fun.

A special trip I do recall from before I was seven years old, was going to Adelaide – from Pt Shields Airport (near Pt Lincoln) to Parafield Airport, as an unaccompanied passenger. The plane was a DC3 and I sat in a single seat in the left side row. At the time I did not know what the occasion was, how it was afforded and how I was to get to and from the airfield in Adelaide. It was possibly early September in '52. Dad had gone earlier with the van full of work and family things with Mum & Marie coming later by ship. Apparently Mum was pregnant and was travelling to Adelaide in case there were complications from her polio. It seems the pregnancy was unexpected and that may explain some of the idiosyncrasies that came with Billy – the only name he was known by, by all, during his childhood.

I am informed that William Donald – named in honour of Opa and Uncle Charlie, (my family was always a bit strange about names) arrived with his umbilical cord around his neck. My memory is of staying with Aunty G, and attending the Eden Hills Primary school and learning about the stolen generation as some of those boys were in my class. I have no idea how we returned to Tumby a few weeks later. There Billy grew with a diet of his own determination. I think he had toast and vegemite for breakfast, as did the rest of us, but he frustrated Mum as for lunch and tea he had little other than white bread and butter topped with fritz and sauce.

Dad and Mum believed in consistency in rearing their family. By way of example Marie and I were given new bikes at the Christmas before we entered grade 3. In later years, it was a watch at the Christmas before starting High School. Another time, Marie had not had a birthday party, I think she had been sick, so when my time came that year we had a double birthday party.

While Dad was involved in the RSL and Freemasonry, Mum belonged to the Church Mother's Union. Her activity was once a month in the afternoon while Dad's activities were as often as weekly, so we became accustomed to Dad being away one night a week for work and another for his social activities. Marie and I had a lot of freedom. I wandered, or cycled from one end of town to the other and rode out into the country. Marie played a lot with the girls from nearby families. There were some rules in place like, I could not go swimming with goggles and snorkel until I could swim from the Jetty landing to shore. This took me a few weeks and then I used a low tide (not mentioned when I boasted of my achievement).

I think there were over twenty kids in my class at school, and probably nearer thirty in Marie's. Each year the school was receiving many more new students than it had previously. We were the first of the notorious Baby Boomers.

I was supposed to come straight home from school and certainly by sunset. This rule was broken on occasions when a travelling circus or rodeo came to town. I would inevitably be delayed and would offer to help them set up in the hope of getting a free ticket for the night's show. A couple of times, or more, Dad would come and drag me away when it was dark. I would be told off and then, if I had a ticket be allowed to go to the show but always accompanied by Dad.

From time to time Dad would be away for several days at a time as he visited more remote areas. Mum was able to join Dad on these trips by farming me out to friends so that I could go to school. Marie would go with them. On one occasion they visited the farm at Minnipa. I recall a couple of occasions where I went with Dad and we would stay with one of the farmers *he had got to know. On an occasion or two Aunty E would stay with Marie and I while Mum and Dad visited the further regions of the West Cost.*

It would probably have been alternative Christmas that we went to Adelaide. I can recall sleeping in a hammock on the veranda at the Aunts' house in Eden Hills. One year I was given a water tommy gun – I had wanted a larger – probably more expensive – water rifle. Another Christmas we stayed at RSL House in the city. Alfa Laval's office was just down King William Street. Dad was a happy drunk after attending the Alfa Laval Christmas party and afterwards, met up with Uncle Reg, our step grandfather, who was similarly disposed. His place of work was a couple of doors further down King William Street.

I recall a concerning event on one trip to Adelaide. We had left home in the company ute quite early one morning. I believe we were only a family of four but we could well have been five. We had been travelling on a dusty road with bends and rises and dips. There was also the occasional cattle ramp. I imagine it was toward year end. Our luggage and some Alfa Laval gear was in the back under the tray cover. Prince was on top of the cover. I looked through the back window. There was no Prince to be seen. I guess I put on a turn and yelled this information out. Dad gradually brought the ute to a stop and we got out to examine the load and road. Still no Prince. A three point turn was executed and we travelled back, what seemed to me to be miles, and I was expecting to find a dead dog. I was not a happy chappy. I doubt if we covered more than a mile or two when we found Prince trotting along the road in the direction the ute had been going. He was uninjured apart from a heavy graze below his jaw. The supposition was that he had slid off as Dad took a corner. I was much relieved as he was my constant companion. We resumed our journey and I think that for the next part Prince joined us in the cabin lying at Mum's feet.

It was decided that the fourth child would be born at the Tumby Bay Hospital. This caused Mum considerable concern. She liked the local GP, who would be in attendance, but was very concerned, that if it was a boy, the Doctor would not circumcise the child. Mum was very much of the opinion that circumcision was appropriate given the climate, sand & dust. I did not know what circumcision was but recall Mum discussing it with her friends at the kitchen table. Fortunately, Elizabeth came, so circumcision was not on the agenda – however when I was sent out to tell friends of her safe arrival my firm instructions were to say 'Her name is Elizabeth, and we will not be calling her Libby.'

Marie and I can recall many summer evenings spent having a picnic tea on the beach. We however, then had to wait for an hour before we were allowed into the water for a swim. That was the belief at the time to prevent drowning. Usually our repeated "Is it time NOW?" resulted in a swim after an extraordinarily long forty five minutes. I have a suspicion that the evening swims were in part determined to overcome two white haired pale skinned kids getting another round of sun or wind burn (that which we got after spending hours near naked outside on hot overcast days). Marie usually got it worse and the curative solution, of the day, was to have a methylated spirits face washer run over her burnt area. She was not a happy girl.

During swimming from the jetty it was not uncommon to see a stingray swimming below. I found that a bit scary and would go as fast as I could to the jetty landing. I do recall seeing seals and once a whale when we were jetty fishing but never a shark. That is until one morning I was heading alone to the jetty for a swim only to see a "humongous" shark hanging from a frame near the foot of the jetty. In truth it was probably around three meters but that was more than twice my height. It seems a teenager had just waded in to go spear fishing when he saw the shark. He aimed and fired his spear gun and got the shark, then managed to land it on the sand. With help he then strung it up. I forwent my swim and returned home to tell of the shark.

At the southern end of the bay a tidal stream separated Tumby Island from the mainland. I was constantly warned to never swim there or cross to the island due to sudden returning rapid water flow. I adhered to this rule. This was probably just as well for I recall two brothers from school, just a little older than I, who were drowned in a similar situation in the next town north.

It must have been toward the end of 1955 that Dad was asked to move to the mid-north/lower Flinders Ranges. The transition was not smooth and really tested Mum out. Without having a new home in sight, the trust home was sold to a couple who had rented it while we were in Adelaide for Billy's birth. The six of us spent the summer living in a small caravan in the local caravan park. At one stage we four kids all had the mumps, or some other similar childhood ailment. Mum found that time very trying, and I recall her retelling the story in later years. After school returned, we moved into a nearby shack. Like the little one bedroom cottage in the Adelaide hills, where Prince first entered our lives, it was of fibro asbestos cladding and of two rooms and bathroom. It however was quite roomy. Marie and I rode to school in the morning but usually made our separate way home. While the search for a new location was still on and well into the year, Dad was advised by Alfa Laval, he could stay at Tumby Bay. This news, to Mum, went down like a lead balloon. The house had been sold and we were living in a two bedroom shack. I do not recall Dad ever going away house hunting, certainly Mum did not. She had no transport of her own. She was looking after four kids aged about six months, three, seven & nine years old.

However after five or so years in Tumby we did a final pack up, said a farewell to friends and our many classmates, and headed of, in midyear, in the newer panel van to Melrose.

CHAPTER 11

Melrose

Melrose is a tiny village at the foot of Mt Remarkable in the Flinders Ranges, about 160 miles north of Adelaide. The children and Sally had never been there before. Jack had only visited it briefly to get his bearings. Driving in, the scenery was beautiful. It was winter. Everything was green. The mountain range was impressive, by Australian standards. There was water in every creek they crossed coming down from Port Augusta. All hope and anticipation.

The day they arrived was cold and wet. First on the agenda was to get a fire going in the house they had managed to rent. The house was about 100 years old and adjoined the Bottom Pub. On the other side was a garage. As it turned out, the Bottom Pub no longer had a licence and was just used for accommodation.

The Top Pub was the one that the towns folk drank at. The old house was owned by the people who owned the garage. No house could be found to purchase, so the family was at the whim of a landlord again. Still, it had two bedrooms and a sleepout for the boys. It was a pretty basic set-up which no longer phased anyone in the family. The toilet was an outhouse down a rather long path in the back garden. Wood stove, chip heater, open fireplace. Sally was pleased to note there was electricity. Not much else about the place pleased her. There was one major difference with this town though. They had relatives there. Jack's half sister, from his father's second marriage, lived on a farm outside town with her husband and five children. The oldest two were of a similar age to George and Marie. Sally was hopeful that this would help their transition to a new school.

It did not help. School for Sally's two oldest children was fraught with disaster. They had come from classes of around thirty children in each grade. The tiny school at Melrose had only about seventy children all up. Mostly farm kids as the town population was only made up of the banker, the policeman, the garage mechanic, a teacher or two, the Publican and the family who ran the bakery/general store.

Grades were combined for ease of teaching and the curriculum seemed far different to their school at Tumby Bay. All classes started the day with a spelling test. Both George and Marie scored 18 out of 20 on the first day. But it was eighteen errors out of twenty words. Not a good start for them. George found it particularly difficult as he felt he had missed some lessons and others he had done the previous year. His class (grade 5) was made up of grades 4 to 7. Marie, in grade 3, was in a class of grades 1 to 3. There were only the two teachers. Billy was still eating fritz sandwiches for breakfast lunch and tea and Lizzy was not even walking yet. The Melrose experiences of the two younger children proved to be very different from the older two.

Right from the start, George had trouble with the male teacher who was in charge of Marie's class. This teacher had three of his own children at the school. Two in George's class and a younger one in Marie's class. It appeared to George that he was always thwarted by these three children. The girls in his class got him into trouble a lot, and although their father taught the other group, George seemed to come off second best for fairness. Even the younger son of the teacher was given privileges which traditionally went to the older boys.

But for Marie, this same teacher inflicted a ruling which would haunt her for much of her life thereafter. He deemed that she could not progress to grade 4 the following year and was to repeat grade 3. Sally was furious. How dare he hold her daughter back. She saw absolutely no reason for it and was even more offended than the child herself. Sally might have deferred to her husband in most matters, but when it came to her children, she was vehement in her search for fairness and justness. And of course, in those days, repeating a grade had a rather bad stigma attached to it.

Sally determined to have Marie seen by a child psychologist. There were two problems with this. Firstly, it was never clearly explained to the child that her parents did not think she should be made to repeat, and they thought the psychologist would prove it. Marie thought her parents believed she had a learning difficulty and they were disappointed in her. The second problem was that the psychologist was in Adelaide and by the time an appointment was available, the school year was half way through. And yes, the psychologist agreed that there was no reason whatsoever that Marie be made to repeat. She was a bright and intelligent girl.

Somewhat lacking in self esteem perhaps, but then, she had spent many months of her life in hospital suffering from eczema, the scars of which haunted her pretty face.

They say that one teacher can make a difference in a child's life. Usually it refers to a good teacher bringing out the best in a child. In the case of George and Marie, this one teacher stole what was left of Marie's self esteem and turned George from a confident, well balanced boy into one who seemed to no longer trust those with authority and become withdrawn into himself.

Billy was oblivious to all this and was fast becoming everybody's favourite. Even his siblings adored him. There was something about that boy which seemed to make him immune to trouble in the family. Even when he started school himself, he just seemed to sail through. In fact, he would sail through most of his life untouched by tragedy, bad luck, misadventure and the sufferings of those around him. Even in his self-centeredness, everybody loved him the most.

The baby grew, and by the time Billy started school, Lizzy was an independent three year old. Sally had gained work at the local general store/bakery. She was able to take both Billy and Lizzy with her. Billy spent a good deal of his time in the bakery annoying the baker until he started school himself, and Lizzy just wondered around the shop, or town for that matter pretty much by herself. It was a very small town. One street. The playground was just across the road from the shop and home. In truth, the whole town looked out for her. Her favourite part was accompanying her mother on the weekly trips to outlying farms to deliver groceries. This meant meeting the locals and playing with their children in the very short time they had together while stores were exchanged and new orders made. Sally drove the store kombi van. It was rugged country and often they passed through rushing creeks and up steep mountain grades. Fear did not seem to be present in the girl. She had absolute faith in her mother. She was also somewhat spoilt, being the baby of the family. She got everything she wanted. Fortunately for her parents, her wants, as befitting the family budget and lifestyle, were small.

For a while there, Sally relaxed. Everything was pretty much in order. Her job at the shop supplemented the family income considerably. The older three children were settled at school and now George was at high school. He took a train to get to the next large centre and although much quieter than he used to be, was still very independent. Lizzy was a dream child. Sally still had no means of transport of her own, but living in such a small town, she didn't need it.

At about this time, the family seemed to advance up the societal strata by a notch or two. For some reason, this particular town held a very well outlined positioning for its citizens according to social standing. All farmers were at the top and those who had farmed for successive generations were at the apex. Next came the essential services people – the stock and station agent and the banker. Next was those such as Police Sergeant, Postmaster and teachers. Others who belonged to multigenerational families in Melrose came next. Lastly there were the "others". Sally and Jack belonged to the "others". They were a little more accepted because Jack's sister had married a local, though only a second generation farmer. Plus, in amongst all that, there was the Protestant Catholic divide. At least the family was of the Protestant majority. Sally was by no means a snob, but hers was one of the founding families of South Australia. Her great, great, great, grandfather, Robert Thomas, had brought out the first printing press to Glenelg in 1836. Subsequent generations, as stated previously, had all done well for themselves.

That is, till her father lost the family fortune trying to be a farmer. Not entirely his fault Sally now conceded, but the family fortune was gone, only the house in Eden Hills remained. Jack did not come from such solid stock, but that sort of thing was not important to him. What was important was his wife's happiness. He set about improving himself. He had already studied bookkeeping in Tumby Bay and was a member of the Freemasons Lodge and RSL. Jack had a knack with words and was occasionally asked to contribute to speeches made by other, better educated men. He also took on the role of Secretary of the School Council. It was still very much the time of being a "Man's world". Sally's innate intelligence went un noticed and un recognised. Even by herself.

Let us not forget the "trouble with her nerves" following her bout of Polio. Life might have had a good dose of family stability to it, but it was by no means easy for her. Jack was still away from home a lot visiting areas further afield for his job. On one occasion he was sent back to his old area of the Eyre Peninsular and was away for eight weeks. Her best ally at this time and on other absences of her husband, was her oldest child. George took on extra duties. Marie would help with the laundry folding. She remembers folding a huge pile of nappies for the baby and not receiving any thanks from her mother. George was sometimes sent to the local shop to buy a bottle of "BCM", This was colloquially known as Better Cure Mum. It contained phenobarbital which was used to treat anxiety at the time. It worked by calming overactive nerves in the body. It is now a controlled substance because of the potential for abuse and dependence. In those days, it was an over the counter tonic!

Towards the end of 1959 the family rented a farmhouse with a square mile home block. It was about four miles out of town on the same road as the cousin's farm. By now there was a bus service to George's high school, but the town school bus service took children from five miles plus out of town. Marie and Billy would wait for the bus nonetheless, and if there was room, they would climb aboard. If the bus was already full it would not stop for them and they would have to walk down to their aunty's house and catch a ride with her children in the car. Sally still had no car of her own and of course, Jack was in the company ute. But on the whole, life on this little farm was a happy time for everyone. Sally felt more in control, unless Jack was away for weeks on end. They acquired 3 milking cows which were machine milked every morning. Any cream surplus to requirements was sold to a local dairy to be churned into butter. They found a goat, a doe, naturally called "Nanny". Sally milked her in the mornings by hand. It was hoped that goat's milk would help with Marie's eczema. No one could define for certain if it did, but one thing they were sure of was that the goat would eat anything. When she ate the skirt cover from Marie's bike she was thereafter tethered to a peg in the middle of the yard. There was a pig, very friendly and just for fun. A couple of sheep periodically wandered in from some other farm. They became quite tame and George was even able to get on the back of one if he was feeling very brave. There were budgies and canaries and a one winged magpie. Sadly Prince had done the last round up of the children and had died of what old dogs die from. He was replaced by Pixie, a small Australia Terrier. She was a much loved pet, but not the companion George had enjoyed for most of his life. There were an assortment of cats from time to time and even a couple of white rabbits. These rabbits caused great hilarity one day when they became caught in the vegetable patch. Sally went in to retrieve them. Rabbits are very quick, especially when the farmer's wife is trying to capture them. One found its way back through the "invisible" hole in the wire mesh by which they had entered. The other gave Sally a merry chase around the lettuces and carrots. Sally was already giggling with memories of Beatrix Potter's Peter Rabbit. She lunged at the little thing and grabbed something soft and white. She held up her hand to the children's screams. It was only the rabbit's tail. The rest of bunny disappeared through its escape hole in the fence.

At around the time of the Royal Adelaide Show, there were annual trips to Adelaide. Parents and two kids in the cab. The two older ones in the back of the ute under the tarp rolling around with milking equipment, spare parts and family clothes and bedding. There were also regular visits from great aunts, old friends and an assortment of cousins. Jack taught George how to use his rifle and how to trap rabbits. There were lots of chooks for eggs and chicken dinners. Rabbits were sold by George, after dressing, for pocket money. The skins were sold in Adelaide on annual visits to the grandparents. These annual visits also occasioned Jack the opportunity for sales meetings with his firm and the after meeting booze up which was part of the deal. At home neither parent drank much. A bottle of beer on a hot day and a shandy for Sally. There was cooking sherry, but it really was just for cooking. Wine was a novelty and not well handled by Sally as the children very quickly referred to it as "giggle juice". Lots of bowls were played by Jack and the occasional round of golf by both of them. Sally never played bowls. Well, she did once, in Tumby Bay, when Jack first took up the sport. She beat him. She never played again. The older children learned to play tennis on Saturday afternoons and Billy did whatever he wanted to do. Lizzy was always a free range child but in her limited way being only four or five by this time. George, the solitary child took off on his bike on every possible occasion. He learned every track and trail in the area. He would be gone for hours. Occasionally there was a telephone call to Sally advising her where he was and could he stay the night please? Life was still a battle for Sally, especially when Jack had to go away to the outer limits of his area, but she had become content with living on a rural property again.

In September of the 5th year the family had been living in Melrose, Sally's happiness at the time came to a resounding end. The day had started as it usually did with her milking the cows then the goat and finally tramping through the pig pen up to the chook yard to feed her "girls" as she called them. Jack usually left for his rounds of farm visits at about 7 o'clock.

This morning however, when Sally got back to the farmhouse to make the school lunches for the older three children, Jack was sitting at the kitchen table having a second cup of tea.

'Are you feeling OK Dear?' she asked. She had never known Jack to be ill, but she had also never known him to break his routine of leaving the house at seven o'clock in the morning either.

'I'll drop George at the bus stop and then take Marie and Billy into school. I need to do some business in Melrose. Then I'll come back for a cuppa and a chat.'

Dread flowed through Sally's body. This was so out of character for Jack. Not at all normal behaviour. They had a simple life, but it was one of domestic routine. She felt in control in this house. The children were happy. Once the older three children had caught their respective busses for school and Jack had left for his visit to whatever prospective client he might have planned, she had the day to herself. Lizzy was an easy child to care for and mostly entertained herself. She had a good imagination that girl. Something bad had happened with Jack's work she thought. Sally was sure of it, but now, with all the children here, was not the time to discuss it.

'Alright.' She said quietly. 'I'll let the kids know they don't have to walk to the bus stop.'

The next two hours were harrowing for her. Why was he taking so long? Her stomach churned, her head ached, her hands shook while she washed the breakfast dishes. Sally had got herself into such a state that she had to run outside to the dunny to throw up. After that episode, she resolved to get about her daily tasks and not think of anything other than what she was doing at the time. She made a fresh batch of scones and set the table with some of last year's apricot jam and yesterday's freshly made cream. The cream reminded her of Jack's job. He must know every farmer from Port Augusta to Clare, she thought. He was a good man, but an average earner. Probably too nice a bloke to make a good salesman. She had always thought that.

Eventually Sally heard the ute pull up at the house.

'What is it?' she demanded. 'Don't ever do that to me again. Going off and leaving me to wonder what is going on. Couldn't we have talked about this last night?' This was the closest she had ever got to shouting at her husband. They were a quiet couple. A quiet family. No shouting and very little raised voices. Not like some of the rellies who just seemed to scream at each other all day.

'I've been posted to the south east.' He said, ignoring her temper and her stress. It was fully justified he knew. He had behaved badly leaving her like that.

'Dairy cows are the second biggest industry down there. Next to pine plantations. There are two dairy factories in Mt Gambier alone, and a few at some of the other towns. It's a good area Sally. But most importantly, the bosses say I will not need any more trips away from home. Everything is pretty much within driving distance from Mt Gambier.' He gently pulled her into his arms. His arms were the safest place she knew.

'How will we tell the kids?' she asked after a moment's reflection. 'They are so happy here. Remember how hard it was for George and Marie when we first came here? I mean, Billy won't mind, nothing phases him. Will Lizzy have to start school not knowing anyone at all?'

'We'll make it exciting for them. A brand new house, a brand new school. And they can jump in puddles because it rains quite a bit down there.'

'Will there be a brand new house and a brand new school?' she asked sceptically, remembering last time such a promise was made.

'Yes. There are new three bedroom trust homes for sale in a new area. They are completed and ready for occupation. There is a new school not far away which is opening next year. George will have a bit further to go to high school, but you know how he likes to go off by himself.'

And so it was done. Again, the decisions made with no input from Sally. Most of the animals were sold or given away. The family packed up and headed to Mount Gambier. The house they bought in that town was theirs for the next fifteen years.

CHAPTER 12

The hill behind the house

Mt Gambier was big enough to be called a city. It had suburbs, four primary schools, two high schools plus a catholic primary school and high school. Every Christian denomination had a Church and there were probably a few Muslim and Jewish people, although Sally's family never met any of them. The main industries were dairy cattle and pine plantations. The volcanic soil was rich and moist. Although there were no rivers in the area, there was an abundance of underground streams. People used to say it rained for nine months of the year and dripped off the pine trees for the other three.

The house which Jack had purchased was in a new development at the northern outskirts of the town. Two streets further north were farms. Two streets to the west was a hill which appeared vacant. The street leading to it ended abruptly. An ancient gum tree sat right on top of the hill. The rest of the land was just green pasture. No-one seemed to own it. That is to say, as far as the local children were concerned, no-one owned it. It was their very own huge playground. Perfect for flying kites. Excellent for running go-carts. A paradise for playing cowboys and Indians. No-one ever worried about their children so long as they were home by five o'clock.

A new primary school was built about half a mile from the house. Roads were not completed and to access the school, some children had to climb over a stile in the fence at the end of the last street of houses.

The main street of the town ran East West and cut the town in half. As with a lot of towns, it also divided the social strata of its inhabitants. The rich people lived to the south. The poor people lived to the north. The children of the town were unaware of this divide and simply chose their friends as children do all over the world.

There was a reasonable amount of road traffic. It was a large town. But this was a time of only one car per household for those who could afford a car at all. When Sally's family first moved there the green grocer truck came by twice a week, the baker every day and the milkman every day including on weekends. If the housewives did need to go into the main street, it was only about a half hour walk from pretty much any-where. Children either walked to school or rode their bikes. Neighbours chatted over the fence and everyone knew everyone else's business. It was a typical, orderly, large country town in a rich agricultural district.

CHAPTER 13

How Jack thought about their life in Mt Gambier

*T*he yard was a mess. I had seen the house previously, when it was still under construction. Close to finish, but not quite. The yard was bare earth and building materials. My heart sank because I knew Sally would be upset. And she was. I could tell from her fallen face as we pulled into the what should have been the driveway. There were weeds and thistles everywhere. Not a bit of dirt was showing.

I had promised Sally and the kids a brand new house in this new town. A brand new school for the three youngest and a well equipped high school for George. The house was definitely brand new, but I knew that all Sally could see when we first pulled up in the old work ute, was the thistles.

A year later, you would not recognize the place. Roses bordering the front garden with a lawn in progress.

Fuchsias down the side of the block next to one neigh-bour. A garage for the car and other junk. And the back yard, well, such a clever girl my Sally. She had designed the back yard into three sections. The part closest to the house was for lawn and play area. The middle section was for veggies and a future chook yard. The back section was reserved for a compost pile and vine type veggies and berries. The garden was still a work in progress, but my goodness that woman could work. Almost every day, while I was out visiting pro-spective clients, she was out there planting, weeding, preparing. On the weekends we would work together to get the heavier things done. I think she eventually forgave me for disappointing her again, about having to start from scratch.

So this small suburban house was our home for the next fifteen years. I liked it. Three bedrooms, kitchen and dining room combined big enough for the six of us. A decent size bathroom so long as only one person at a time used it. The toilet was out next to the laundry, but still within the house proper. The sitting room was large enough for a couch and a couple of arm chairs plus the piano. Bit of a squeeze, but it did fit. The boys had one bedroom, the girls another and Sally and I had the biggest one. The kids were used to sharing anyway, so that was not an issue. Family life was good and Sally seemed content enough for a while. I adored that woman. I would do anything for her, but she never asked me to do anything for her. I'm not sure if it was because she could do pretty much everything herself, or whether it was because she didn't want to be disappointed in me. I know I wasn't the best salesman and barely made enough money to support the family, but I did do my very best.

Still, as the children grew and expenses became higher, it was pretty obvious that we were not doing too well. I remember when we proposed putting the kids on the "free" list for books etc. at school and Lizzy burst into tears. Apparently she was of the opinion that only poor people went on the free list. She was right of course. We were poor people. The kids just didn't realise it because Sally held things together so well. In the end, Sally solved the problem of not enough money. She bought a grocery shop.

I had left Alfa Laval by this time. They wanted me to travel again to a bigger area and I just couldn't put Sally through that trauma any more. I changed jobs and worked for one of the local real estate firms valuing and selling farms. I got my real estate licence and valuers licence. In Mt Gambier there were only two real estate firms at the time. One was owned and operated by a very independent woman Miss Gebhart. She was a feisty one, but for some reason she respected me, even though I worked for the other firm. That was owned by a chap who's wife Sally liked and they had four kids too. Similar ages to ours. Anyway, this Miss Gebhart lent us the money to buy a small grocery shop. It was the days before supermarkets. Each suburb had a small shopping centre with a butcher and deli, maybe a hair dresser or a green grocer. The grocery shop we bought was on the other side of town, about four miles from home. There was our grocery shop, a deli, a butcher, a green grocer and a hair dresser. Today the shop might be called a mini mart or something like that. Anyway, during the week and Saturday morning, Sally was at the shop and I continued trying to sell real estate. We used to count the cash together every night, but it was definitely Sally's project and she took it very seriously. I found a retired book keeper through the RSL and he used to keep track of the finances. He told me that Sally was always trying to sell goods for 1c less than she paid for them in order to keep her customers. In truth, we didn't make much of a profit, but it did keep us in groceries and with bartering, meat and green gro-ceries. We didn't need a food budget for the family.

The kids loved the shop, especially the younger two. They would go there most afternoons after school and play in the cellar in the cardboard boxes, or would weigh up bags of sugar to put on the shelves. Marie was taught how to operate the till so she could cover for Sally sometimes, but I don't think she liked it.

We would have been one of the very few families in those days where both partners worked. In retrospect, it would have been hard for Sally because she still had a family of six to cook for every night, school lunches to prepare and all that washing. I eventually talked her into getting someone to clean the house once a week. We also changed over the wood slow combustion stove for a gas one. Likewise the sitting room fire and the hot water service. There was a new debutant dress for Marie when she turned sixteen and a couple of ball gowns. I think Lizzy even got the occasional new dress. Mostly it was Marie's hand-me-downs or clothes from the op-shop. Mind you, Sally was an excellent dress maker and she passed that skill on to Marie, and Liz when she got a bit older. The old Singer sewing machine got a good work out on weekends.

I played bowls on Saturday afternoons and many Sundays too. When the boys were playing hockey on Saturday afternoons I got to see some matches. There was the RSL and Lodge. I liked spending time in the garden. I took up woodwork and made a few things for the house. At some point I decided that I wanted to do public speaking. There was nothing wrong with my speech and I had always been a stickler for correct grammar and didn't swear or even use much slang. Someone at Lodge suggested I join a Toastmasters Club. So I did, and I enjoyed it very much.

George was a strange boy. Getting a conversation out of him was like extracting teeth. He left school at sixteen at the end of his Leaving year and got a job at a local shoe shop, but immediately applied to work at Softwood Holdings. That was a big timber producing and processing company in The Mount. When he turned seventeen he got accepted into some kind of training program with Softwoods. George had a plan for education apparently, and was going to get that through Softwoods. He volunteered to join the army a bit earlier than if he was called up for National Service. Did his training at Puckapunyal and then served in Vietnam. Thank God he came home. But he was even more withdrawn than before. He was a man now, but still grunted like a teenager when asked a question. The job was waiting for him at Softwoods when he returned from the army. True to his plan he married his sweetheart as soon as they turned twenty one. Then he started studying by correspondence. He went on to get a University degree in something or other. I was very proud of him, but didn't know how to tell him.

Marie did not have a plan, so Sally and I made a plan for her. She seemed to be struggling at school, or rather, hated tests and exams. She got very nervous. So rather than her finish intermediate at fifteen, we organised for her to leave school earlier than the rest of the kids her age. She got a job straight away and started growing up way too fast for my liking. There were a few boyfriends which Sally and I managed to keep an eye on. Then there was this young lad from New Zealand who wormed his way into our home. Marie was crazy about him. But one Sunday morning I caught him sneaking out of the girls' bedroom. I don't know how long he had been in there, or what he was doing, but I sent him packing and told him to never come back. Pretty soon after that Marie joined the Army too. She was posted to Melbourne so that left just Billy and Liz at home. Then Billy went to Adelaide to study and that left Lizzy.

Lizzy was the youngest and probably we spoilt her a bit. She was a pretty independent little thing. She would take herself off to the pictures or the swimming pool or the YMCA dances. She never needed a bunch of girlfriends to do these things, just went by herself. I remember one time I really upset her though. She was about eleven years old at the time. There were regular Saturday night dances for pre teens at the YMCA. I was to pick her up when the dance finished at 10:30. I was a little early, so walked into the hall to watch the kids dancing for a while. I saw Lizzy dancing with this boy I didn't know, but he looked OK. But when she saw me her face turned to thunder. She left the poor boy in the middle of the dance floor, picked up her handbag and came storming over to me. She got into the car and turned her head away from me and would not speak. The next morning she still had the sulks with me and wouldn't talk. Up to this point, she had adored her daddy, but I was certainly getting the cold shoulder now. Then Sally suggested I take her out to a farm I was in the process of valuing. Smart girl my Sally. I know I've said that before, but she really knew what was going on with the kids. She knew that Liz liked drives in the country and also knew that the girl would realise it was my way of trying to make up to her. I rang the chap at the farm and said I was bringing my youngest daughter out and if there was any possibility of a horse hanging around it would stand me in good stead with the little girl. Well, not only was there a horse (a very old Shetland pony) but it was all saddled up and quite used to strange little girls who had never ridden a horse before. The pony took Lizzy for a walk around the paddock, all by itself and I was back in the good books with my daughter.

I never had that kind of relationship with Marie though. Looking back, I realise that we were a bit hard on her. Myself in particular. She left home early and I suspect it was to get away from Sally and me and our hard parenting. We expected a lot from our kids and I guess we thought they should behave the way we wanted them to behave which was, pretty much the way we were made to behave when we were growing up. But of course, times change and I did not. Well, not for George and Marie anyway. I had softened a lot with Lizzy. Billy just did whatever he wanted to do and managed to keep it within our boundaries. Well, what we knew about anyway. It wasn't till years after the fact that I discovered he and his mate had dug holes in the back yard. Anyway, back to Marie. About a year after she joined the army she met a bloke, also in the army, and brought him home to meet us. This was clearly a serious relationship but I quite liked the young chap. He seemed a decent sort. I sort of thought *that the army would take the role of parents and make sure that no hanky-panky was allowed to happen. I was wrong. Soon after Marie brought Bob home to meet us, she told us she was pregnant. I felt betrayed and very disappointed. I took it all out on Marie. She and Bob had already said that they wanted to marry, but I thought they would leave it till Marie was twenty one. She was only nineteen at this stage, Bob was a few years older and had already done one stint in Vietnam and another in Malasia. He was permanent army, not a nasho.*

It was obvious that the wedding would be brought forward. We made Marie actually ask her big brother George's permission to get married before him. Then I insisted there were to be no frills at the wedding. No white dress, no hymns, no dancing. Basically I made the girl feel ashamed, and soured our relationship for life. As it turned out, she lost the baby before the wedding, but the damage was done. Marie never forgave me for treating her the way I did. Fortunately she had chosen a good bloke and they went on to have four great kids and a long and I think happy marriage. I was wrong in the way I treated my oldest daughter. Especially as time went on and as Lizzy was growing up I was a lot more lenient with her, but, she also left home at an early age.

Well, Lizzy would say that we left home. You see, because I was a lot older than Sally I was well into my forties when Lizzy was born. And when I turned sixty I was forced to retire from my job with the firm I was working for at the time. I had done other courses with that company and really enjoyed working for them. But, big business being what it was, and this was a very big South Australian company, they restructured and everyone over fifty was retrenched. I tried a few odd jobs in the Mount, but I just couldn't stick at it and I think Sally was ashamed of me being unemployed. We still had Liz at home to support. There was work to be had in Victoria where Marie and Bob were living at the time. So we organised for a young working couple to live in our house and look after Liz while she finished her last year of high school. Then the next year she got a job in the bank and she shared the house with two other young women. They were both teachers and very respectable. But the thing is, Lizzy became independent both financially and emotionally. She took up with this long haired git. Sally and I moved to Adelaide and organised with the bank for Lizzy to be transferred there. She got married as soon as she turned eighteen and went back to The Mount to live. But in her case, it was Sally she was trying to get away from, not me so much. Sally was really struggling emotionally at the time. We had lost our first grandchild. Marie and Bob's daughter. She was only three years old. Then, I guess I couldn't sell to save myself and Sally started a whole new career with Social Services. She was fifty years old. Not a good time for any woman I'm told.

Like I said, times changed, but Sally and I could not see it. We could have done a lot better by our kids.

CHAPTER 14

Did Jack have an affair?

Sally and Jack were a very conservative couple. They were also pretty typical of couples in the '60s. They struggled financially, but made the best of things. Sally was very good at stretching a meal before she bought the shop. After that there was always plenty of food. A healthy diet for her family was her first priority. They were a good looking pair as well. Before she turned grey, Sally's hair was a dark brown tending to auburn. She was a little above average height, held herself well and always dressed to the best of her budget, which was always very small. She had a strong intelligent face. Jack was tall and had a full head of dark hair. And he was one of the nicest blokes one could ever meet. He was popular in the bowls club, popular in the RSL and popular with his Lodge colleagues. But, he was an innocent.

While they were living in Mt Gambier, Jack's brother, full brother that is, same mother and father, lived in Western Australia. He was also a Lodge member. He was going to be inducted as the Grand Master for that state. This was a very important event in the Freemasons Lodge society and for a man's family. Jack would have liked to attend, but there simply was not enough money to afford the trip. Word got about, as it does with such organisations, and a sponsor was found. The lady in question was a widow of a past member. She was held in very high regard in Mt Gambier society. She came to visit Jack and Sally on a couple of occasions before offering to pay for Jack's trip to Western Australia to stand by his brother. Now this was a very generous offer by a woman previously unknown to the family. The children could not quite understand it. Sally was pleased for Jack, but was a little concerned that another woman was taking such interest in her husband. Was it all above board? She hated her suspicion. She overheard the older kids discussing it one day and gave them very short shrift indeed.

'Don't be so disrespectful. How could you think such a thing!' she admonished them. But in truth, she was not too sure herself. Strangers were not usually that generous.

The day Jack was to catch the plane to Adelaide, and then on to Perth, he took Sally into his arms and held her the way he always had. Nothing had changed. He was her man and she knew then that he always would be, no matter what.

CHAPTER 15

This is how Sally thought about things in Mt Gambier and other musing about her children

I was not particularly pleased about having to move again, this time to Mount Gambier. It had taken me five years to feel settled in Melrose. The only good thing about this latest move was that I hoped it would be the last. At least till the kids had grown up. Jack must have felt that way too because we agreed to buy a house there. No more renting. And it was a brand new house in a brand new suburb with a brand new primary school. Only problem was everything had to be done from scratch.

It was only a couple of years after this move that Jack resigned from Alfa Laval. That didn't bother me, but why he thought he could sell land instead of separating machines was beyond me. To be honest, I knew that I would always have to find a way to supplement the family income. In those days women didn't work outside the home unless they were a professional like a doctor or something. Professional women of the time were also single. No husband and children to look after. In the end, we bought a small grocery shop and that became my project. I didn't ever really make a profit, but I did keep the family in groceries and fresh food from the local butcher and green grocer in the same block as my shop. It was hard of course. Running a family of six people and running the shop five and half days a week. All I can say is I was very tired most of the time. I didn't make as many friends as I used to in other towns. I guess I was just too busy. I left the school P&C and Lizzy's Swimming Club Committee up to Jack. He always liked that sort of thing. And of course he had his other activities of RSL, bowls, bowls and more bowls. Then Toastmasters and I suppose a bit to do with The Lodge. But I don't think that lasted the whole time we were there. In the later years, there was a lot of social activity with The Legion of Ex Service men and Women. There were dances every Friday night and the occasional RSL one on a Saturday. We only had Liz at home then, and she came with us.

She was a bit of a worry. She was thirteen going on twenty three, if you know what I mean.

I was never disappointed with my children. They just didn't turn out the way I hoped they would. Silly me for expecting so much I suppose. Looking back now, that is a really stupid statement "the way I hoped they would".

George married at twenty one which I thought was too young, even though I was married at twenty one. He was the first of many generations to gain university qualifications. He held some very prestigious roles including CEO of one of Adelaide's large private hospitals. He had a perfect wife and two perfect children. He kept an eye on me when I got older and he never moved away from Adelaide where I was living in my retirement.

Marie got pregnant before she married and both Jack and I saw it as such a scandal. Jack was mortified and I was upset because it meant she too would marry young. Jack made her go through a very traumatic time over the wedding and I was just too tired to argue with him. Looking back we were very, very wrong in the way we treated Marie. And of course, probably no-one else in town saw sex before marriage as scandalous. It was the '60s after all. I should have been grateful for small mercies. Marie and Bob gave us our first grand-child. Sharon was truly an angel. She was too good for this world and God took her away from us when she was only three years old. At the time we were living in a caravan in the back yard of Marie and Bob's place in Wodonga. – How we got there is a whole other story. But I should have spent more time with Marie when Sharon died. She already had another baby by then. Jack made me leave. He packed us up and took us off to goodness knows where about two weeks after the funeral. I don't know why he did that. I don't know why I let him. After all these years I still regret not being there for Marie when she probably needed me the most.

Billy, well Billy was Billy. Breezed through life. Never got into any trouble (that I know about). Didn't finish Uni, but made up for it later with other studies. Picked a good woman for a wife. They had trouble having children, but modern science fixed that prob-lem for the first one and then Louise got pregnant with their second while she was breast feeding the first. Wonders will never cease. Of all of my children I thought Billy, or Bill as he called himself once he left Mt Gamber, would be the most successful. Perhaps he was. I don't know really. He never told me much. I do *remember one incident with Billy, but it was long after the Mt Gambier days. I must have been telling him off or giving my opinion about something. He said to me, very calmly, 'Do not wag your finger at me Mum.' Of course, I didn't even realise that I was doing it but I was. I never wagged my finger at him again, or any of the other kids for that matter.*

Lizzy was our youngest and we adored her. Pity she grew up to give us the most grief. I realise now that I raised the boys different to the girls. I know that I suffered the same thing, being just a girl. Why I carried the belief system on I have no idea. It is just the way things were in those times. I myself never really had a teenagehood. I went from being a child of thirteen to being a woman of fourteen years of age. So I had no experience of what teenage girls went through. Somewhere in there Lizzy and I lost communication. She could still talk to her dad, whom she adored, but she simply stopped talking to me about anything personal. Was it my fault? Probably. But it did cause us both a lot of heartache. In the end we reconciled. But I was nearly eighty by then and she was approaching fifty. So many years wasted. It wasn't that we were estranged or anything. We still saw each other, spoke to each other, visited each other. But it must have appeared to her that I did not approve of anything she did. Because, in reality, I didn't. She was just so different. So, getting back to Mt Gambier, Lizzy was an absolute delight, until the day she turned fourteen!

Mt Gambier was the town where we lived through the '60s. Times were changing, but Jack and I were not keeping up. He was a lot older than me and until he turned sixty, this was not really an issue for either of us. He was a lovely man, but not the most reliable. He would sometimes forget to pay household bills. It wasn't deliberate, it just happened. He spent, in my opinion, way too much time at the bowling club. He smoked that pipe everywhere. In the car, in the house, in the club rooms. They didn't know about passive smoking in those days. I started smoking at some stage, but it didn't stick. I suspect Marie stole the occasional packet of smokes from the shop when she thought I didn't know and we did catch Billy and his mates having a puff in the cubby house once. Little sins really. My kids were not habitual thieves or cheats. They all got in to the top stream at high school, even Marie. This was supposed to mean they were above average intelligence. I have no idea where they got the smarts from. It certainly was not from their father.

Liz once said to me, long afterward, 'it was you Mum.', but I didn't believe her.

Living in Mt Gambier did nothing to improve my station in life. I was always Jack's wife or the kids' mum. I had no standing in my own right. It was not really important to me personally. What other people thought was still important though. 'What will people think, Lizzy'? 'Who cares Mum?' Mind you, that verbal response only came when she was past her twenties. Up to that point it was just a blank stare. Which meant the same thing. In retrospect, I did put too much stock on what other people might think. And, as I said before, the world was moving on and I wasn't. Other people were probably not the least bit interested in what went on in my family.

Do you remember the house in Eden Hills? It was such a big part of my life when I was growing up. Summer holidays spent with my Aunts. Sometimes with a parent or two, but always with my brothers. It was there that I met my life time friend Josie and her parents, who really, were much better parents to me than my own. It was also a big part of my children's lives. Some times we would visit there as a family. Or I would send Billy and Lizzy off by themselves to stay with their great aunts. In the later years, Marie spent a *lot of time there looking after one of the aunts. I can't remember if it was "E" or "G". She had baby Sharon with her at the time. At one stage Jack had to go to Adelaide to have ray treatment on a growth on his chin. The house at Eden Hills was empty at the time. Aunty "E" had passed away and "G" was in a home. I sent Lizzy with her father and from all accounts they had a nice father/daughter time. She was his favourite child and he was by far her favourite parent. We all considered the house in Eden Hills as our family home. Apparently it wasn't. It was Gertrude's home, when Ethewin had passed, and soon Gertrude needed full time care. So my brothers, who both lived in Adelaide, put her into a nursing home. This institution was not cheap and the family was expected to pay for the care of the elderly. That meant the house had to be sold. I wanted to buy it. My brothers were not at all interested in keeping it, but I was. I put my proposal to Jack but he refused. He said we didn't have the money. Which, was probably true, but we would have found the money. We could have sold our house in Mt Gambier and moved back to Eden Hills. We would have had to borrow more, but I am sure we could have done it. But he said no. End of story. End of the historical home.*

So I was a wife and mother. My lot in life. The "lot" of most women my age no doubt. I was never one to complain at what life threw at me, but at times I was hurt. Jack quitting his first real estate job was a bad thing. His joining Southern Farmers was a good thing. George and Marie both joining the army so young was a bad thing. Producing grandchildren was a good thing. Lizzy being divorced three times was a bad thing, many times over. But her finding her life partner at forty three years old was a good thing many times over. My ups and downs were dependent on my husband and my children. Never for anything I did myself. I was devoid of action. Devoid of choices. I was programmed to live my life the way I thought others thought I should.

Who were these "others"? My parents? Well they were a big disappointment. The ladies on the school canteen? They were just wives and mothers like me. My brothers and their wives? We had very little to do with them. Probably only saw them three times each in all the time we lived in Mt Gambier. The Church? Well, there's a possibility. I was a regular Church goer. But over the years I think I only did that so that I would be seen to be a good Christian. Many years after Mt Gambier, when I was staying with Marie and

Bob in Queensland and Liz happened to be visiting at the same time, the three of us women got into a religious discussion. 'I've always tried to be a good Christian.' said Marie and I almost in unison.

'What does that mean?' asked Liz.

'Do unto others as you would have them do unto you.' again, almost in unison.

'That is being a good person.' said Liz. ' Muslims and Jews and all religions believe the same thing. Being a Christian is "believing that Jesus Christ was the son of God and through Him you will have eternal life.".' Marie and I just looked at each other. I don't think our faith had ever gone that deep, but clearly Liz's had at some point. Because that was what she was claiming to no longer believe.

I still continued to attend Church. Marie didn't. Lizzy came to Church with me whenever she was staying with me in Adelaide in the later years. She sang the hymns, said the prayers and was respectful to the Minister. But I realise now that she was doing it all to support me. Not because she believed any of it.

So, was my life a waste of time? Probably not. My husband adored me. My children respected me. I loved them all dearly. They gave me purpose when I had none of my own. I just wish I had spent more *time trying to get to know them. To understand them. Instead, I just judged them according to some standard which I believed at the time, but which became more and more irrelevant to me as time went on.*

CHAPTER 16

Did Sally have depression?
Jack simply said "not quite right"

Sally had a strong constitution. After her bout of Poliomyelitis, she was rarely ever ill. But illness, as we now know, goes further than illness of the physical body. These days, asking someone "How's your mental health?" is not considered unusual or even intrusive. It's a bit like saying "Have you had COVID yet?". In the 1960s, things were quite different. People who were considered "loopy" were suffering from some kind of phobia. "Senile" was dementia. "Mad" was almost certainly psychosis in some form or other. And some people were just "sad".

Sally was a mixture of sad, angry, cranky, intolerant, anxious, generally fed-up and very, very tired. Jack put it all in one basket called "not quite right" and he blamed it on the Polio. When he found his oldest daughter crying because her mother had called her a lazy bitch, it was because her mum was "not quite right". When the youngest daughter was labelled a slut, the same excuse was given. So the family tipped toed through Sally's depression. No-one ever thought that she could be helped. They forgave, but did not forget. Sally's sons thought she was a tough old boot. Her daughters thought she was cruel, unloving and definitely hypocritical.

It was not until George, and Marie's husband Bob. who were both returned soldiers from Vietnam, were diagnosed as having Post Traumatic Stress Disorder or PTSD that their respective wives started to see similarities in Sally's behaviour and that of the two men. So did Sally have PTSD also. If so, what was the trauma which she had suffered?

The children and broader family knew of no "Traumatic" event in Sally's life which would indicate an onset of mental illness, except Polio. Can you imagine being flat on your back for eighteen months or so. In hospital. Not seeing your children. Knowing that there was no cure for your disease except "rest". Not knowing if you were going to live through it all. Having absolutely no control over your life.

How little they all knew her. For a clever woman she had no independence until after Jack died. In her early years she took so much responsibility for the family farm only to have her father walk off the land leaving her mother and the children behind. Then there was the time when Jack was serving overseas during WWII and she didn't know if he would come back or not.

Jack's explanation or excuse for Sally's sometimes unusual behaviour was probably correct. "Your mum is not quite right after she had polio". Sadly, if mental health was discussed in those days, she could have got help. But of-course it wasn't. So this woman continued her life knowing she was falling short, but not knowing how to make things better. And all the while, she was trying to do the right thing by her family. The right thing, as dictated by her upbringing, her church, the local society in which she lived, even her husband. But to do the right thing for herself, was never a consideration.

CHAPTER 17

The oldest son remembers Mt Gambier

The Mount was alright I suppose, but I did struggle when we first went there. It was nothing like living in Melrose where I had so much freedom. There seemed to be no rules in Melrose even though I did have more responsibilities, especially when dad was away. In this new place there were rules. Be home at a certain time. Do your homework. Spend Sunday with the family, no visiting friends on Sunday. Go to Church with mum and the other kids. Dad only went to the family service once a month. And even then it was just for show because I knew he didn't really believe in God like I did. But he was very strict with us all. Maybe living in a bigger town made him more protective of his family, but it just looked like control to me. He even tried to control mum. He succeeded to a certain extent. But she was so much smarter than him that she could nearly always find a way round him to get what she wanted. Not that she ever wanted anything for herself, it was just things she wanted for the household or family.

The strangest thing about dad's strict parenting was that he was so quiet about it. There was no shouting or yelling. There was very rarely a smack. I remember dad would sit at the head of the table and keep complete control of his children by holding the bread knife by the blade's tip. And if a rude word was spoken, the handle of the knife would land gently but firmly on the child's knuckles. Billy got more wrapped knuckles than anyone, but he hardly even noticed.

I guess I became a bit of a loner when in the Mount. I had never had really close friends (except for my dog Prince), but in the tiny towns like Tumby Bay and Melrose, I didn't need close friendships. I was too busy exploring, riding my bike, catching rabbits, shooting pigeons and other solitary activities. Except for riding my bike, all other of these activities stopping in Mt Gambier. Even riding the bike was boring because I couldn't go off exploring. Well, I did do a lot of exploring around the lakes that were there, but no one else in the family knew that.

I left school at sixteen when I finished my leaving year. I got a job in a local shoe shop but immediately applied to Softwoods for one of their traineeships. I was accepted when I turned seventeen and settled down to doing what they said as well as what Mum and Dad said. Then, when I was eighteen I met Georgina. She was beautiful. I had known her at school but had not paid much attention to her there. But this was something else. We just seemed to belong together. I really, really loved her. More than I thought it possible to love anyone. Of course, we wanted to get married, but both sets of parents were against it. Not that they didn't approve of us being girlfriend and boyfriend, they just said we were far too young to get married.

So I came up with my first five year plan. The first of many in my life and have basically lived my life according to my continuous five year plans. This plan included a separation from Georgina, then a reconciliation, then building a house, then getting married and starting a family. All whilst getting a university education which was only open to me through Softwoods. So I joined the army, served in Vietnam then came back to The Mount after my two years. That allowed for everyone to see that Georgina and I were serious about each other. My job with Softwoods was secure and with us both now working, we were able to buy a block of land and start building a house. The house was finished by the time I turned 21 and Georgie was just a few months younger. We got married. I commenced my Bachelor of Business by correspondence and our first child was born a bit over a year after we married. Everything according to plan. My Masters and the second child were part of the next five year plan. Also achieved.

To be honest, I didn't have a lot to do with my younger brother and sisters. There was nine years between me, the oldest and Lizzy the youngest. Billy and I shared a bedroom before I left home and he was a little shit, but alright really. I did notice that mum and dad seemed very hard on Marie. She was very much controlled by them and wanted to rebel. But being a girl and not having a lot of self esteem, probably due to the way our parents treated her, she was stuck. It was me that suggested she join the army as a polite and acceptable way to leave home. Lizzy was a different kettle of fish. No shortage of self esteem in that kid. In the end, she didn't have to leave home early, our folks did. They left her alone in the house when she was just fifteen years old. Well not really alone because they had a young married couple living with her and looking after her, supposedly. Everyone thought she was so grown up for her age, but really, she was just a kid, albeit a confident one. They had originally expected Georgie and I to look after her, but it was not part of my plan to be parenting my teenage little sister.

It seemed to me that life was very different for each of us four kids. Billy and I, being boys, had it a lot easier than the girls. And Lizzy had it a lot easier than Marie who was seven years older than her. Marie was the one who suffered the most. I don't think she enjoyed her childhood very much at all. She had suffered a lot with eczema as a little one and always carried the stigma of having to repeat one year in primary school. Then it was mum and dad who decided that she should leave school before the rest of her classmates. They thought she had little chance of passing her exams. Marie was not a bad scholar. It was just that she was nervous of tests. Her innate smartness was proven when she joined the army and got into "intelligence". But that was all for nothing when she got pregnant. Mum and Dad were horrible to her. They made her ask my permission to marry before me. Not that it was any of my business. I knew what was going on but Marie didn't have the nerve to tell me, so I didn't ask her. I just said she didn't need my permission to marry before me just because I was the eldest. And then Dad imposed all these arcane rules, like no white dress, no decorations in the Church, no singing or dancing etc. It was cruel. I just could not think of dad with the same respect after that. They didn't disapprove of Bob of course. Thought the sun shone out of his arse, it was just the whole sex before marriage thing. Unbelievable. I was a committed Christian but I would never have put Marie through that sort of shame. As it happened, she had a miscarriage before the wedding so was not pregnant when they got married. I think Marie has suffered some kind of emotional turmoil ever since. And I vaguely remember that our parents' expectations of Marie and control over her did not end with her marriage.

Bob did another tour of Vietnam when their first child was only a few weeks old. There seemed to be no question that Marie and the baby would come and live at home in Mt Gambier while Bob was away. Marie, Lizzy and baby Sharon all squashed into one tiny bedroom. Marie having to do all the house work for the family as well as look after the baby. She was even sent away to look after an ailing aunt, and she had a three month old baby at the time. I'm glad Georgie and I had our own place. I just stayed out of it all, but I did feel for Marie. I should have told her so. I should have supported her more. I guess I had my own issues at the time and just stuck to the things that were in my own life plan. That I could control myself.

Many years later I was diagnosed with PTSD. So, lots of emotional trauma floating around our family. Lots of things that should have been said but never were.

CHAPTER 18

What happened to George?
Why did he change?

When the family moved to Mt Gambier, George was about fourteen years old. Even in those days, teenage boys were teenage boys, and not much different to subsequent generations. They were rebellious, noisy, forever hungry, moody, very interested in girls and thought they knew everything. George was all of these things, but about ten times quieter about it.

His rebelliousness was wanting to leave school at the end of what was called Leaving, rather than go on to do one more year of high school. He was an intelligent boy. He gave a logical argument for his case to his parents, and his desire was granted. Neither parent was really familiar with the benefits of higher education at the time. It was different when young Bill wanted to continue to the final year of high school and go on to university. But then, Bill won himself a scholarship.

George's noisiness really only extended to his raucous laughter when reading his favourite "Spy Vs Spy" magazines. Not much else grabbed his emotions.

Yes, he had a very good appetite. He ate more than anyone else at the table. No problem with that. He could make his own school lunch sandwiches and never expected his mother or sister to run round after him.

Rather than moody, his parents would say he was quiet. He didn't initiate conversation. Sally in particular noticed that he spoke only when spoken to. He offered nothing to family conversation. He was a good boy, and his mother appreciated that. He was just quiet. In fact, he was very quiet.

As far as being interested in girls, the only girl he showed any interest in was a farm girl called Georgina. He married her when they turned twenty-one and raised two perfect children and stayed married for the rest of their lives.

As a teenager, George did think he knew everything. But he was such a reserved young man that he didn't call anyone to order about it. He had a respectful relationship with his father. If he ever rolled his eyes as teenagers do, no one saw him do it. He performed all his household chores as required. He tolerated sharing a room with Billy. That was always their lot. But at least in Mt Gambier it was inside the house, not a sleepout as it had been in other places. Just as well, because Mt Gambier was very cold during winter. The closeness he once had with Marie faded over the years. He partnered her for her Debut, but only because he was told to. Lizzy hardly knew him at all.

George joined the YMCA soon after moving to Mt Gambier. He was a reasonably athletic boy but the only team sport he was interested in was Hockey. YMCA offered a few other options like gymnastics. They also held regular dances for children and teenagers of various age groups. Marie and Billy also joined, and much later Lizzy would end up teaching swimming there after a new complex had been built later in the 60s. Because her children were all involved in this association, Sally joined the committee. She was a very community minded mother. She was also a rather intelligent woman with not much opportunity to shine.

So how did this outgoing, overconfident, totally fearless boy in Tumby Bay turn into such a quiet person? Was it that horrible teacher from Melrose? The one who was so unfair. Was George bullied at school? Possibly. He had a very strong sense of right and wrong, what was fair and unfair. He would always stand up for the under-dog. Excellent qualities in a person, but how does a school boy fair in the playground? Whatever it was, George made a conscious effort to leave childhood behind as soon as he possibly could. Of Sally's four children, she would admit, but only to herself, that George turned out the best. But she did worry about the change in his personality when they moved to Mt Gambier. As the boy became an independent man with his own family, Sally worried less. He did seem to be managing his life quite well. However, there were at least two nervous break-downs, or they were called that at the time. Sally knew what people meant by that, because she had been there herself a couple of times. But this young man sought help. He was a return serviceman. A Vietnam Veteran. And there were options open to him which were not open to his mother or his grandfather. Once he opened up about his experiences in Vietnam, he began to heal. But Sally always wondered if there was more to it than his war experiences. As his mother, she noticed the change in him much, much earlier than his young adulthood.

CHAPTER 19

How was life for Marie in Mt Gambier and her early adulthood

Mmmmm. What can I say. I'm hunting around my memory bank for some good bits. There must have been some. I remember my best friend Jackie. The two of us girls got up to a lot of mischief our parents didn't know about. In retrospect, I was very grateful for that friendship. Without Jackie I think I would have turned into a complete non-event. I seemed to be totally controlled by my parents. Older brother George became more and more distant as we grew up. Little brother Billy was a pain in the backside, but I adored him anyway. My little sister Lizzy was a blessing. She seemed to worship me. There was seven years difference in our ages, so we were never friends as such, but she was a source of comfort to me.

During our early years in Mt Gambier, we often visited our Grandmother and Uncle Reg in Adelaide. I will always remember the sound of the white gravel footpath under our feet as we walked down the side of the house. Almost every time we had a family get together there, the good silver-plated cutlery would come out of the drawer where it was kept. Mum was always upset about that cutlery set. She would mutter something like 'that should have been mine' whenever Grandma was out of the room. I didn't get the full story till many years later. It's an interesting story and does explain some of the tension we all felt between Mum and Grandma. I wont explain it here. But I hope someone does.

My friend Jackie very nearly didn't turn up at my wedding, and she was my bridesmaid. I am not even going to talk about my wedding. It was probably the worst day of my life. Not because of my husband. Bob was great, but because of all the rubbish that Dad and Mum put me through before hand.

I used to play a lot of basketball. Also, later in life had two knee replacements. I was not brilliant at school, but probably better than Mum and Dad thought I was. I had a couple of decent boy friends. And a couple of not so decent ones. Mum and Dad were pretty good at controlling me. Well, they thought they were. I was smart enough to get away with a few things they didn't know about…. But let's not go there either.

I thought I had got away from The Mount when I joined the army. But when Bob was sent to Vietnam again and I had the baby I was very quickly brought back to the family home. Bob and I were stationed in Melbourne at the time and it was assumed I could not manage by myself. I would have, given the chance. Still, I didn't mind so much sharing my old bedroom with Lizzy and baby Sharon. Lizzy was besotted with the baby as was the rest of the family. But with both my parents working and Liz and Bill at school I was left alone and expected to do all the housework, washing and cooking for the entire family. If it had just been my own little family I would not have minded, but it was everyone.

Fortunately Bob was back after a year and we were posted to Wodonga in Victoria. An army wife is not a glamourous job. But I did make friends with other women in the same situation as me. Another baby, a boy this time. And then tragedy. We lost Sharon. She was just three years old. We had taken her to hospital to have her adenoids out and she didn't wake up from the anaesthetic. How can a beautiful little girl like that not come home? At the time, Mum and Dad were living in a caravan in our back yard – another story entirely, but they were there and that was helpful. I think. We also had our baby boy and he was a distraction. But to be honest, I think I lost a year of my memories around that time.

In the early years at Wodonga, Lizzy was still living in Mt Gambier and our parents were moving around the country seeking work for Dad. They still had her to support after all. I was a bit jealous of her. She seemed to have a lot of freedom for someone so young. She was only fifteen when the folks left her there with a young couple to look after her. She was doing a secretarial course at high school. That year she started going out with a teacher from another school. Alarm bells were ringing all over the place but nothing was done. She got a job at the end of that year and the romance fizzled out. The following year she shared the house with two young female teachers. So in reality, she was physically and financially independent from Mum and Dad. Good for her. Lucky girl. The next boyfriend was not a respectable teacher, but, according to Dad, "a long haired git". Such was our parents thinking. This time they took action. They moved back to South Australia and rented a house in Adelaide. Dad got some sort of job but it was Mum who was really earning the money. Anyway, they arranged for Liz to be transferred with the bank she worked for. She was just seventeen at the time and really had no say in the matter. They hauled her off to Adelaide to live with them. The relationship between Mum and Liz went completely down the toilet. She could still tolerate Dad because she still adored him but he was no help to her. This romance continued, despite the separation, or maybe because of it. Lizzy announced that when she turned eighteen she would be returning to Mt Gambier to live with Jeffrey. Mum and Dad could not conceive of her living with a man. They said she might as well marry him them. So she did. The week after she turned eighteen, as promised, no parental consent being required by then. If they had just let her do what she wanted, the relationship probably would have fizzled out too, and Lizzy would have been spared a whole lot of heartache.

CHAPTER 20

The things Marie could not talk about. Who broke her heart?

If George was an atypical teenager, Marie was archetypical. She was sulky, dreamy, rebellious and loved boys. Problem was, her mother had never really been a teenager and didn't know how to handle her. As for her father, well, there were rules for boys and very different rules for girls.

So how does a teenage girl, who wants to be part of the popular group at school, manage in such a conservative family. Not well. She had the usual crush on the pop idols of the time. Some of her friends were even allowed to go to Melbourne to see The Beatles in 1964. The closest Marie came was to be allowed to put posters up on her bedroom wall. Beside Paul McCartney she also loved Gene Pitney and Roy Orbison. She would have a sneaky cigarette with her friend Jackie, in the park, halfway between their houses. She would dream of meeting someone and falling in love. Now that her eczema and acne were clearing up, she was quite an attractive teenager. She played a lot of basketball and went to the YMCA Dances. Once she turned sixteen, she was allowed to go to the Barn Palais dance, so long as it was with her older brother. This dance was an institution in Mt Gambier. Over the years it went from a big open hall with a stage for the band, to a rather up-market restaurant with international acts.

The boy-friend thing was difficult for Marie. She was what they call a late bloomer, but once she had bloomed, she was beautiful. Her father watched her like a hawk. In order to get past the parental control she and her friend Jackie took holidays together to stay with family friends in other towns. There was a holiday in Tumby Bay, staying with old family friends that Sally had kept in touch with. She met a boy there. There were frequent short stays with Jacky's grandparents in a small town half way to Adelaide. She met a boy there. And then there was the boy from New Zealand. The one Jack kicked out. Finally there was the soldier she met in Melbourne whom she married and lived happily ever after with. Some dreams do come true. But my goodness there were a lot of tears in between time. Marie shared her bedroom with Lizzy. And even though she was seven years younger, Lizzy knew her big sister was hurting. A lot. She was even crying the weekend she came home from Melbourne to put her trousseau together before her wedding. What was that about? Lizzy knew Marie was not sad about leaving home for good (or what she thought was for good) but something very sad was chewing away at her beautiful big sister. It was not till Lizzy was much older that she was able to recognize a broken heart. But who had broken her sister's heart she was never able to say.

CHAPTER 21

Billy looks back at growing up in Mt Gambier

When I was about seventy years old, and about to enter retirement, I told a good friend that I had the best and happiest childhood I could ever imagine.

In those days, the '60s, kids were pretty much unfettered. I was a very happy kid and thought life was a breeze. I had no idea of the things my sisters went through and not a great deal of interest in what life was like for George. He was always so remote from the rest of us. In communication anyway. There was about six years between us and he was already at high school when we moved to Mt Gambier. Not much of what he did affected me, nor, probably my sisters.

Mum was clearly the boss of the family, although Dad, on occasion, tried to pretend he was. He was an odd bloke my Dad. He went off to work every day without complaint. I remember that he changed jobs somewhere through that decade. He used to sell separating machines to farmers, but then he went into Real Estate. It was at about this time that he decided to "improve" himself. He started taking a bigger interest in the Freemasons Lodge, whatever that was. And he joined a Toastmaster club and learnt the art of public speaking. I have a vague memory of him and George taking turns with the reel to reel tape recorder Dad had bought. I was not very interested. Much too busy playing with my Mechano set or building Christal sets that I had hung up on the curtain rod of my bedroom. I think I got better reception there. There must have been some interaction with George, but as I say, he was almost like a different species to me, even though he was a boy. I was much closer to Lizzy. In fact, I adored her, even though she was a girl. Because of the gap between the first two kids and then me and Lizzy, we found ourselves the only two at home for a few years before I went to Adelaide to go to Uni.

I was one of those lucky little shits that got through primary school without doing much homework. I got through high school without doing much study. Then got a scholarship to go to Uni to study engineering.

When I was a little kid I made friends easily. Still do, now that I am in my 70s. I was blessed really, as my sisters have pointed out. Not only was I a boy child, I was everyone's favourite. And I mean everyone. Mum and Dad favoured me over the girls. My grandparents in Adelaide were only too happy to have me board with them when I went to Uni. All my teachers seemed to like me, especially Mrs Ethleston my grade 6 teacher. I think she somehow saw potential in me and tried to get me to pay attention at school in readiness for high school. I didn't really pay much attention and still came in the top five of the class. But some teachers do leave a lasting impression on you. I had lots of friends growing up and some of my high school friends and I are still in contact even after fifty five years. In high school I didn't do too badly with the girls either.

My best friend, before I hit puberty, was Anthony Payne. He lived next door. They were a family of four kids too. Anthony was my age and the oldest. Then came a shit of a kid called Nicholas and then a girl a bit younger than Lizzy. There was a baby who came much later. I think his name was Lance. Their bastard of a father went out for cigarettes one day and didn't come back. Literally did not come back. Deserted them. His wife and four young children. I found out many years *later that Mrs Payne had married again about twelve years after the desertion. She found a nice bloke and lived happily ever after apparently. She deserved it. She did not have an easy time of being a "deserted wife".*

Anyway, Anthony and I got up to a lot of mischief when we were kids. I was a construction engineer even when I was ten years old. My best effort was a hole in the back yard, big enough to hide about three boys. We sured it up with pine planks from the wood shed. There was a concealed entry behind the compost heap. My mates and I would crawl into it and plan all sorts of devilish deeds. The dirt from the hole went over the back fence to a vacant block. The hole was dug sideways, not just straight down. How it didn't collapse was due, as I said, to my engineering skills and the pine planks we stole from dad's shed. It wasn't discovered till a few years later when dad and mum installed a gas heater and we didn't need the wood shed anymore. Dad dismantled it and was putting all the spare timber in the back corner of the yard.....behind the compost heap!

Then there was the saga of the cubby house. There was an old chook yard with a very sturdy coop. As a lot of things in that area, the original coop was built, by Dad and older brother George, with limestone blocks. So when the chooks all departed this earth we converted the coop part of the chook yard compound into a cubby house. All good, lots of family involvement. Dad and I did it together. We put in a ceiling under the peaked tin roof. Added a door which could be closed. Installed timber plank flooring. It was quite a luxurious cubby house, you could easily fit five kids and a bit of play furniture. So the rules were, that one day would be girl's day when Lizzy and her friends could use it and the next day would be boy's day when my mates and I would use it. I was probably around twelve or thirteen at this time because I was becoming interested in girls. Not really wanting to have anything to do with them, but wanted to know how they worked, so to speak. Anyway, the boy girl alternate day arrangement worked very well for a few months when one day, Lizzy and her friends heard strange noises coming from the ceiling of the cubby house. We were discovered. Anthony and I had built a secret man hole in the ceiling and when we knew the girls were going to have a meeting in the cubby house, we would sneak down there and hide in the cavity and spy on them. I actually don't think Lizzy dobbed us in, but the game was up and we could never hide up there again.

Things got quite busy as I entered my teens. Like I said, I didn't need to try too hard at school, and there were a whole lot of other interesting things to occupy my attention. Girls. They were no longer curiosity objects but quite interesting play things. I don't mean that in a derogatory way, but back then, in the '60s, girls were designed to be kissed and not taken too seriously. And in high school, I never did more than kissing. But I did kiss a lot of them. I might have tried to go a bit further, but I had a great deal of respect (for a teenager) for females and if a girl said no, I stopped. They all said no if I tried to advance past kissing.

Learning to drive was a big thing for me. Dad taught us all except for Lizzy. We had this family car which was universally referred to as The Old White Holden. I think it was a Holden EK. I think it died before Lizzy was old enough to drive. Somewhere along the line, Dad bought a huge Dodge Desota. It must have been from the 1950s but could still do 80 miles an hour down the airport straight! Not that I ever told Dad that. I remember driving it all the way to Sydney when I was only about seventeen. There was Mum and Lizzy and Oma & Opa. We were taking the oldies to Sydney to visit their daughter and two grandchildren. Mum got very ill along the way and I had to take over driving. We just rolled her out of the car and into a hotel in Canberra, rolled her back into the car the next morning, then continued on from there. There was also a trip to Melbourne for Marie's wedding with Mum, Dad, Lizzy and me. I don't remember much about the whole thing.

Being the clever little shit that I was, I applied for, and gained a scholarship to help with expenses to attend Uni. Uni was in Adelaide and the plan was that I was to board with my grandparents. I lost my scholarship after the first year of Engineering. Not to worry, I worked in the pine forests near home during the long summer break and saved enough money to cover another year at Uni. After the second year I gave up and got a real job. Uni was somewhat different to high school and I guess I had never really learnt the art of studying. Still, that job lead to another job and so on. All in the construction industry. And I did go and get my full qualifications as a registered builder. I just took my time about it. I never was one to hurry anything.

In my later working life, I ended up teaching other would be builders at TAFE. Weird really, to go full circle from student to teacher in the building industry. I never imagined I would end up being a teacher aged *over sixty. But really, it was an easy gig. Well, it was till I ran foul of the bureaucracy of TAFE. Another story.*

CHAPTER 22

This observation is from Liz when she and Bill were much older

As you know by now, life in general came easy to Billy. And on top of that, he was popular. He was the favourite of all his family members, grandparents included. He was popular at school. Head prefect in his final year of high school. He was intelligent, fair minded, charming, genuinely interested in others. Although he was very self centred there was an innocence about his selfishness. He was not malicious. His selfishness was purely a reflection of the attention he received. He met most of the goals he set for himself, and if he didn't he would casually find another way to get what he wanted. After failing to keep his scholarship at Uni, he went about supporting himself for another year. He spent two hot summers at the top of those pine forests, watching for fires.

Other boys in their late teens were doing far more interesting things. And some were doing nothing at all. He gained most jobs he applied for. He was head hunted by one large construction firm in Adelaide. He was a registered builder in his own right. He joined The Young Liberals. He flourished. He married the only woman he ever wanted to marry. An equally intelligent young woman a couple of years older than him. They had much in common. When they were unable to make babies on their own, they got help and achieved the required result. Two wonderful little boys, very close together. Job done.

But I always felt there was something lacking in Billy's being. Or rather, that he felt there was something lacking. It seemed to me, particularly when I grew up, that Billy had the feeling he could have done better. Could have achieved more. He wanted more. He wanted better. But what was it that illuded him? Was it a spiritual thing? He had tried Christianity, didn't like it. He dabbled in Buddhism, not bad, but not quite "it". He had Jewish friends and understood the religion well. But that wasn't it either. He studied Islam because so many of his workers were Muslim. He was a good leader and truly wanted to understand other people. So perhaps it wasn't a spiritual thing after all. Perhaps it was a political thing.

Billy had political aspirations in his early twenties. It made for great family dinner conversation. George was a die-hard Labor supporter and Billy was just as passionate about the Liberals. Dad took a back seat. Mum served tea. Marie and I left the room.

The difference between my two brothers was that one was a planner and the other was a drifter. The planner had no political ambition but the drifter probably did. He just didn't know how to make a plan to achieve his goals. Those plans would have included taking chances and drifters don't consciously take chances. Planners do. George achieved everything he set out to because he planned to. Bill drifted from one good place to another, but it was not the place he really wanted to be. Because he didn't plan it, and he did not take chances.

It was not until both Bill and I were in our forties that Bill happened to mention "I could have been Premier of South Australia." I let the conversation slide, but I now knew what it was that had been irking my adored brother all those years.

How the baby of the family, Lizzy, saw Mt Gambier

When I left Mt Gambier, sorry, when I chose to leave Mt Gambier, I swore I would never go back. And except for a quick passing through visit to my old school friend Carolyn, I never have.

Actually, I enjoyed growing up in Mt Gambier. The rift between the town and me came much later. I was a pretty independent kid and didn't really need the company of other girl friends as I was growing up. But I did have quite a few. I was a very organised little girl and used to plan after school activities for my friends and I when we were in primary school. I remember we formed a kind of club called the daffodils. We used to climb the big willow tree in our front yard and sing this little song "We are the Daffodils uh haa". We were silly little girls, but we had fun. We had shared use of the cubby house in our back yard. Girls' day for us one day. Then Boys' day for brother Billy and his mates the next day, and so on. I would say that Carolyn was my best friend back then in primary school and early High School. In fact, my brother Billy was probably my "bestest" friend. Or was it just that we got along really well? I once overheard Mum telling a friend of hers that we just used to talk to each other for hours. Even today, Bill is my most loved and best friend!

I became a swimmer in about grade 6 or 7. Back-stroke was my best stroke. I held the girls 50m backstroke record at my high school in my final year. I was very keen on the swimming club. We only had a 33m public pool in Mt Gambier but none of us really minded. I used to ride my bike to training in the morning, train for about an hour, ride home, have breakfast then ride to school. And I have to tell you, this was Mt Gambier, freezing cold at 6 o'clock in the morning, even in summer. No training during winter because it really was too cold. High school became a source of some angst. Lots of home work, lots of study, lots of boyfriends. I gave up swimming club and piano lessons to concentrate on my studies. Not that it got me where I wanted to go. I wanted to go to the Institute of Technology in Adelaide and study science. I wanted to be a commercial scientist (whatever that was). I had previously wanted to be an actress but knew that was just a dream. I was in the top stream at school. Can you believe we were even taught Latin! Pretty sure I failed Latin in my final year at that school. I only just scraped through French which I did rather like. The thing was, the subjects I was learning were directing me to university studies. But I knew there was no way my parents could afford for me to go to Uni. I would have to board in Adelaide like brother Billy. But unlike brother Billy I was not the favourite grandchild and could not bear the thought of living with my grandparents. Dad didn't seem to have a real job at this stage. They never involved me in any financial discussions, but I knew that money was very short, even with just me at home. I discovered that the other high school in town, known as the Tech school, was offering a one year secretarial course. This would at least equip me with skills which I could use in the workforce. Not much call for French and Latin and advanced science in Mt Gambier. So I changed schools for what was my fourth year at High School. Everyone thought I was very mature to make that decision. Really, it was the first of many brave decisions I had to make in my life in order to survive. I did the course and had a job waiting for me in the bank as soon as I finished my final exams. I was sixteen.

When I was much younger my big sister got married. She was in the army at the time and had met a really nice man, also in the army. I used to look forward so much to Marie's visits home on leave. Even if they were only for a few days. I missed her terribly when she left for the army. The only benefit was that she handed down to me all her clothes that she no longer needed. They were a bit old for me, but I loved having so many choices. Anyway, back to the wedding. At one of these regular visits she and Bob announced their engagement. I can imagine that Mum and Dad expected them to wait till Marie was twenty-one. Bob was a few years older. Then suddenly the wedding was brought forward. She bought a lovely yellow dress suite. I was busy looking through Marie's wardrobe and could see she already had a couple of white dresses. If money was short, surely she could wear one of those? No, it had to be a new outfit to get married in. Buy why yellow? She liked yellow, I think is what she told me. The wedding was to be in Melbourne where both she and Bob were posted in the army. But I did not know that she had already left the army. And why couldn't she get married here in Mt Gambier?

Some other logical reason was given. Her best friend Jackie was to be her bridesmaid. There was to be only one bride's maid. Mum, Dad, Billy and I drove over to Melbourne for the wedding. I don't remember George being there, but he probably was. He was back from Vietnam by then and he was going to get married himself, later in the year.

It was many years later that Marie told me why she couldn't have a white wedding dress. I was horrified. Not at Marie, but at our parents. 'If it's any consolation', I said to Marie, 'Mum wouldn't let me wear white for my wedding either. "In case the priest asks you a certain question"'. I just gave a sneaky smirk and chose a cream brocade and made my own dress. By then, I spoke as little as possible with my mother. She had hauled me away from Mt Gambier and my boyfriend and made me live with her and Dad in Adelaide. I was just counting the weeks till I turned eighteen and could return. Mum said later that she reckoned Donny Dunstan, the current Premier of South Australia, changed the law, so that people could marry at eighteen without parental consent, just for me. Not true of-course, but I was extremely grateful for the change in the law.

As I said, I enjoyed growing up in Mt Gambier. I had a loving family. Mind you, there was not really a whole lot of cuddling and certainly no "I love you". But I did know they all loved me and that is what is important. Mum did seem to be cranky all the time. Dad was my hero. He seemed to have a charmed life. Mum seemed to work, work, work. I don't remember her smiling much. Except, there is this one photo. A family picnic on the side of the road, which was a regular occurrence in the early years of Mt Gambier. Mum and Dad are sitting on the grass and he is looking at her. You can just see the love coming out of him. Mum is smiling and has a contented look on her face. I still have that photo. Somewhere.

I haven't said a lot about George. He is nine years older than me and was not really part of my life in Mt Gambier. I remember when he joined the army. He was sent to Vietnam of-course. They all were. The year that he was there I remember crying at school on ANZAC day. The teachers were making much of the sacrifice that our young men were making in Vietnam. They didn't realise that one of those young men was my big brother.

Although pretty much absent from my life, George was there when I needed him. I needed him when

Marie's little girl died. George and I were her God Parents. Marie had chosen us because at the time, we were both committed Christians. George remained so. I did not. He was there when I needed to escape from Mt Gambier and get away from the idiot I was living with. I had left my husband for this idiot. Out of the frying pan into the fire as they say. George helped me move and I stayed with him and Georgie for a week or so till I could organise a transfer in my job to Adelaide. There were many other fry pans and fires after that. But not in Mt Gambier.

I know that Marie mentioned The Silver Cutlery Set, but you didn't get the whole story. I feel I can tell it now as much time has passed. My Grandmother has also passed.

When Jack was working at another farm in Minnipa in 1938 he won a cutlery set. He was able to play golf on his days off. His boss at the time, Bill Morrison, liked to play at the Yaninee Golf Club. This was only about five miles from his farm, and he didn't particularly want the locals from Minnipa to know how bad he was. So he was very happy to take Jack along to have a round or two. It improved both their games. It improved Jack's game so much that he was entered into a regional tournament. Now the region was not particularly large, or noteworthy and certainly not affluent. Most of the greens at the local clubs were maintained on a voluntary basis by members. Jack won the competition. He was first in a field of twenty five. The prize was a silver cutlery set. Now this particular cutlery set was not an everyday item in the district. It had been donated by the son of a recently deceased member of the Wudinna Golf Club. The old chap had the set in his family for generations. It was far too good to use, according to the wives of the various descendants of the original owner. It originated in England way back in the late 19th century. There was documentation inside the ornate wood box, lined with blue velvet, holding the sixty eight pieces. It included fish knives and forks, plus some serving spoons. One picture showed a drawing of the original premises proclaiming Sir John Bennett was clockmaker to the Royal Observatory. Established 1750. The guarantee, signed by Sir John Bennett stated that the "Royal Sandringham" spoons and forks are heavily Sterling Silver plated on the finest quality Nickel Silver. The exclusive Silverware was hand finished. There followed instruction on how to clean and care for the silverware and the box in which it came. Thus ensuring the items *should last a lifetime. Well, it had already lasted several lifetimes before Jack was presented with this prize.*

Jack gave the set to Mabel for safe keeping, not having a home of his own. Besides, he knew that he was going to marry Sally when she was old enough, so he would eventually get the cutlery set back. Really, the thing was way too posh for comfort for this country boy.

The cutlery set stayed with Mabel and was never handed over to Jack and Sally after they married. Mabel seemed to think it was hers. It came out for special occasions when the extended family gathered round the dining table at Mabel and Reg's place. Every time this happened, as soon as Mabel left the room, Sally would whisper to the child sitting next to her, but never to Jack himself, that 'That cutlery set should be mine'.

After dinner Lizzy and Billy would set up Chinese checkers on the sitting room floor. Reg and Jack had a scotch and Jack would light his pipe. Sally, Mable and Marie would go to the kitchen to do the dishes. There was frost in the air. But Marie didn't notice. She felt privileged to dry the pieces of cutlery and carefully restore them to their box. Each had its individual mold in the box. Then the box was returned to the top drawer of the dining room sideboard.

Over the years Marie and I were able to get out of our mother the whole story. It seemed to gnaw at Sally's sense of fairness that the cutlery set remained in the possession of her mother, not her. After all, it was in fact her husband who originally acquired it. Jack himself, never mentioned the cutlery set. These whispered conversations were had outside of his hearing. Jack was not the least bit interested in antique table settings. What was important to him was that he "got the girl". She was sitting there right next to him with all their children.

It was not until Mabel and Reg's house was sold, to pay for their aged care accommodation, that Sally eventually got her hands on the cutlery set. But by this time, Jack had passed and all her children grown and spread themselves out all over the country. And it was a very short tenure. Bill's wife admired the cutlery. Louise was the wife of the much adored favorite son, so Sally gave them the set. Had Bill known the history of the cutlery set, which he did not, he might have protested the gift. Certainly Louise knew nothing of its history. She thought it was simply "Grandma's silver cutlery set". But Bill, as we know, would have completely missed the significance of the beautiful cutlery set.

CHAPTER 24

Let's examine Lizzy

Although Lizzy was the perfect youngest child, she grew up to be the most confused of the lot. She would be dubbed the black sheep of the family. The girl most likely to succeed, didn't. Well, not for a very, very long time.

Directly across the road from the family home in Mt Gamber was a vacant block. This was subsequently purchased by the Baptist Church and a new modern building was erected. On Sundays it accommodated church services and on various evenings it was a youth fellowship club, bible study hall and community hub. Lizzy joined the Youth Fellowship Club. None of her friends came. It was one of the many solo activities the child took up. Sally was not too impressed. As far as she was concerned, there was only one religion and that was the Anglican Religion, Church of England. But it seemed a safe enough environment for her daughter. There were games and sports and yes, a bit of bible bashing but it all seemed OK. That was until Lizzy went on the annual October Camp and came home declaring that she had given herself to Jesus!

The Jesus thing lasted a couple of years, by which time real boys were taking His place. She had lots of boyfriends. Quite literally one would be ringing the front door-bell while another was leaving by the kitchen door. Lizzy was only thirteen at the time and her mother had the attitude of "safety in numbers". Lizzy wasn't quite sure what was meant by that. She did kiss most of these boys, but she had no intention to letting things go any further. She didn't know what "further" meant. It was not until Sally realised that the kissing was limited to one boy only that she became quite concerned. She had cause to be concerned. Lizzy found out what "further" meant when she was fifteen. Strangely enough, the whole Jesus thing, and having a steady boyfriend did in a way keep Lizzy safe. While her friends were stealing lipsticks from the local shop she was horrified and retreated to the company of her boyfriend. She never took drugs. Never drank alcohol. Never got pregnant. Having a much older, wiser boyfriend sorted that out.

So, when did the black sheep appear? It was a gradual thing really. At the age of sixteen she found herself fully independent. She had a good job at the Bank. She was sharing her house with two other women. She attended church, either the Baptist or United Church (brother George was United Church) on a reasonably regular basis. She had a steady boyfriend and her parents lived in another state. Had she been left to her own devises she may have matured, ditched the boyfriend, advanced in the bank, discovered that banks didn't promote women so changed direction to someone that did, found another boyfriend, or two and eventually married at 23 and had a tribe of kids who were all equally as successful as their imaginary father. But life did not go like that. Her parents disapproved of the current boyfriend and took her away and made her live with them in Adelaide. She rebelled. She turned black and started to Baa.

The only way she could get away from her parents was to marry the boyfriend. She did, and of course it was a mistake. She could always get a "good job" as her mother put it, but she would always leave said good job in pursuit of some other man. She followed the next husband all the way across the country. Things did settle down there for a while. She started studying to improve her career chances. They had two gorgeous children, boy first, then a girl. But things were not right and she didn't have the courage to tell her mother that she was being controlled by her husband. Lizzy only knew that she seemed to have one personality for home, that of perfect wife and mother. Another personality at work, and another personality when she attended classes at TAFE. No-one had even coined the term "Coercive control" at that time. All she knew was that her husband was treating her very, very badly. There was no physical violence, but what she experienced would make a perfect coercive control case study for those who wished to explore it. She managed to get away, with the children, one night when her husband was so drunk he couldn't get up the stairs to abuse her.

The next husband was a decent sort, but she was never in love with him. It only took Lizzy two years to figure out she had married him for all the wrong reasons. Sally was not impressed with him either. She could see control there again. What was it that men always wanted to control this girl? It was no wonder she didn't really know who she was.

One day she packed up her children and her possessions and moved from NSW to Perth. The city where brother Billy lived. Not to Adelaide where her mother or the children's father now lived. She took back control of her own life. She took a risk and it paid off. She took up university studies, advanced in her career and eventually met her Mr Wonderful.

CHAPTER 25

A reflection on 1972

Lizzy was sulking in her bedroom. She did this most weekends. Sally and Jack had rented a house in Adalaide and had brought Lizzy back from Mt Gambier to live with them. She was not happy with this arrangement. In fact she was miserable, angry and offended. Quite a lot of negative emotions, but she was still a teenager and that can be confusing for anyone. For some reason, her brother Bill had decided to leave his share house and live with his parents as well. He was not asked to, or even hinted at why. Whatever his reasons, Lizzy was incredibly grateful to him.

On this particular Saturday, Jack came into Lizzy's room in a state of agitation.

'I can't find your mother.' He said. 'She's not in the house and she has been gone about an hour. She does not just wander off. Come and help look for her.'

Lizzy could see from her father's demeanour that he was truly worried. The last time anyone had seen her mum was at lunch time. Reluctantly, but with a little bit of concern, Lizzy put on shoes and jumper, met with Billy and her dad and had a brief exchange. It was decided that Lizzy would walk round the block and Billy and Jack would look along the river bank. The Torrens flowed a street away. It was not parklands, but quite dense bush on the banks. Lizzy's stomach started to churn. Why on earth would her mother go down there? She got the very distinct impression that this was not a time for questioning, but for action.

Jack and Billy found Sally about an hour later. She had been down on the banks of the river and had clearly been crying, but was uninjured.

The usual silence fell over the family. It was not until the next day that Jack took Lizzy aside and tried to explain things to her.

'Ever since your mum had polio she has not been quite right. And then with Sharon dying and now not being able to talk to you and then her boss wouldn't give her time off for Bill's 21st Birthday Party. Plus, she is fifty years old and that is a difficult time for women.' Really, Jack was a man of few words, but he managed to get the message across pretty well. It took a little while for Lizzy to realise, but she thought her dad was trying to say that her mum had considered suicide. The word was never spoken of course. Not then. Not ever. But the incident was never forgotten. Bill and Liz spoke of it occasionally in later years. And many, many years later, Lizzy realised it was a sign of depression in her mother. In those days, people didn't know about depression. Jack would only ever say "not quite right". Or "very upset". All of these things were true. Sharon's death had effected Sally almost as much as it had effected Marie. Sharon was the first grandchild. She was Sally's hope for the future. And to be taken so young was completely without comprehension. And yes, Sally was going through menopause and believed that no-one loved her. Her self worth was zero.

Then there was Lizzy. It was like having a stranger in the house. Not a very nice stranger at that. The girl had completely withdrawn from her mother. There had been cross words when she announced that when she turned eighteen she was going back to Mt Gambier and would live with Jeffrey. In Sally's mind, and in

Jack's even more so, having their daughter "live in sin" was totally unacceptable.

'You might as well marry him then.' Said Sally.

'OK. I will'. Was Lizzy's reply. It was what she had wanted to do anyhow.

Shortly after that, Jeffrey presented her with an engagement ring and they started making wedding plans. This was difficult because Jeffrey lived in Mt Gambier and Lizzy in Adelaide. They saw each other about once a month when Lizzy would go back to see him and "stay with Jeffrey's parents". She didn't of course, she stayed with Jeffrey in his flat. But to put a spanner in the works for Sally was the fact that Jeffrey's family were Roman Catholic. The whole thing was a mess really. It would have been so much easier if Sally and Jack had just supported the kid in living with her boyfriend. Couples did that in those days. It was the start of the "try before you buy" era. Lizzy knew at least three friends who were doing this. And although she did want to marry Jeffrey, she realised a few years later that if her parents had supported her in living with him outside of marriage, she would never have married him. The relationship would have been over in a year.

The wedding was held in Adelaide but in a Catholic Church. Afternoon tea was provided by Sally and Jack at the house they were renting. Lizzy made her own wedding dress. A simple style from cream brocade, (not white) and Sally knitted her a beautiful long coat with hood to go with the dress. It was a sign of the love Sally had for her youngest daughter that she did this. Her hands were so painful with arthritis at times she did not know how she was going to get the thing finished.

Lizzy went back to Mt Gambier and shortly afterward Bill returned to a share house with his mates. It was just Jack and Sally alone after all these years.

CHAPTER 26

Jack and Sally alone

By this time, Sally was fifty one years old and Jack sixty four. Still too young for the aged pension. Jack was entitled to a small amount as an ex-service-man if he was officially retired. He was still trying to sell something or other. Commission only. Sally would just shake her head in disbelief every time he came home with another commission based job. She didn't discourage him of course. She was always the support-ive wife. Afterall, Sally always knew it would be up to her to bring in the bacon at some point in their lives.

She had joined the Department of Community Services when they moved to Adelaide. She described herself, on her job description as "Cook/Domestic". She was assigned to what was colloquially labelled as "a bad girls' home". Really the girls living there were not necessarily bad. They were just teenagers. Most with no family to look after them. Some whose family did not want to look after them and some who had offended but not badly enough for juvenile detention. Unfortunately, being teenagers, Sally found it difficult to relate to them. Her experience with her own teenage daughters had not served her well. And, as she was never a teenager herself, she had little understanding of these girls. She could cook and clean though. Her wife and mother role stood her in good stead with those skills.

Life was almost boring for a year or two. The money was adequate and the job a breeze. She quite enjoyed cooking for a big family again. There were about ten girls and three staff at that particular home. Sally's only concern was an increase in Jack's coughing. His pipe was still his constant companion. She had stopped fretting over her own children. They seemed to be ticking along quite well without her. Marie and Lizzy made regular Sunday night phone calls, as did George. George and Georgie were still living in Mt Gamber. Billy popped into the house occasionally. He never rang beforehand. He didn't make a regular thing of his seeing them. Just impromptu visits. Sally wasn't sure if it was his parents he came to visit or the piano. He would turn up, play the piano for about an hour, have a cup of tea and then leave. Still, beggars can't be choosers.

It must be noted, that South Australia at the time, and for decades previously and afterward, was very good at providing public housing, or affordable housing. The pair had purchased their homes in Tumby Bay and in Mt Gambier from the South Australia Housing Trust. The Trust built houses for rental and for sale. Lizzy and Jeffrey were renting a very nice house in Mt Gambier. Sally and Jack were eventually allocated a two bedroom unit in one of the southern suburbs of Adelaide. Everyone had to go on a waiting list of course, but it was only a year to eighteen months long. The unit they got was in a complex where most of the other tenants were either retired, or approaching retirement age. There were well maintained public grounds and their own small back yard. Sally set about planting out that small garden. She had fruit trees and shrubs, flowering bushes and perennial flowers. There was a garden path and outdoor chairs and rows of pot plants on elevated stands. Jack gave up trying to find work once he turned 65 and was granted an ex-serviceman's pension. Sally was working full time and really quite enjoying it. She made a few friends and found a new church nearby. Sadly, Jack's health was deteriorating and he no longer played bowls. He had a passing interest in macrame or 'knot making' as he called it. But mostly he sat in his chair, smoked his pipe and coughed a lot! He was a lovely man though. Sally quite liked having him all to herself. They both appreciated each other's company. Jack's love for his wife had not diminished one bit. He still adored her. As for Sally, well, she loved the old coot.

It was soon after they moved into the unit at Christie Downs that Sally was approached by her boss at one of the homes she worked at for the Department of Communities. Sally had known Mary for the past two years and had come across her a few times at various meetings and residential facilities. For a while there, Sally was on the "relief" roster, so spent a week here and a week there filling in for permanent staff on leave.

'Meredith.' (Sally used her real name when introducing herself. "Sally" was reserved for family) 'Do you think you would like to undertake some training with the Department? I think you would make a good Residential Care Worker. It is a more senior role and obviously pays more, quite a bit more than your current rate for a cook.'

'I've not really thought about it.' replied Sally. 'Would there be much involved?'

'The Department would take you through a few courses. Bit of psychology. Bit of trauma care and de-escalation techniques. You know that some of these kids have been through hell. We really need someone to help out in the homes which have kids with disabilities. Those poor kids have been given up by their families, for what ever reason, and they need someone with compassion to take care of them.'

'Compassion?' queried Sally. 'Do you think I have compassion?'

'Yes.' Replied Mary, with a half smile. 'I've seen you trying to interact with some of the kids and you have a different approach to a lot of people. You don't judge them. You just accept them for who they are. I know you say you don't understand teenagers and I've heard you talk about your own kids. But that was different. You had expectations of your own kids which you think they didn't live up to. But I've noticed that you don't have expectations for our girls. You just accept them and do your best for them. I heard you trying to teach young Emily how to put stockings on the other day. No-one else has bothered to do that. Mostly, if a child doesn't know how to dress themselves we just let them figure it out themselves or just let them look ridiculous. But you care. I think you would be good at looking after these children. Most of them are Wards of the State, and don't really have anyone else.'

'I'll think about it.' replied Sally. 'I'll talk to Jack.'

She didn't talk to Jack. Well she did, but just to say that the Department wanted her to undergo some extra training. No mention that it was voluntary. No mention that her boss had put her up for it. No mention that it would lead to a more responsible, better paid position. This was something she needed to do for herself, by herself. Her husband was dying. She knew that. No need for a doctor to confirm it. Countless attempts by her to get Jack to a doctor had been rebuffed. She had been a nurse for heaven's sake, she knew exactly what was going on. What she didn't know was how long she and Jack would have together. She was only in her early fifties and would have a lot of life after he was gone. She was not going to try to survive on a war widow's pension. And besides, she was up to this. She could work, study and look after her man. She was a woman after all. Women can do anything, given the opportunity. Mind you, she said to herself, some opportunities are not welcome. She always knew that the age difference between her and Jack would catch up with them eventually. She did not want to see her lovely man wither away. Like most of us, she had hoped they would meet a quick exit from this life. But she had watched her aunts live to be over 100. 'Just vegetables really' she had remarked to her children. She did not want that for Jack. And, for Jack's part, he was not as un-knowing as he made out. He did suspect what was happening to him. He knew there was something seriously wrong with his lungs. This was the mid '70s. The word cancer was still not bandied around. He didn't know if he had cancer or not. He had no intention of finding out. He had also seen Sally's relatives linger and linger and linger. He had seen the weekly visits she made to them. Dragging the kids along, well, the girls anyway. The boys refused point blank to go and see old Aunty G and their other great aunts. He had seen his wife take on the major care of her own parents whilst holding down a full-time job. He knew that he would die before Sally, given the age difference. But where Sally was as fit as a fiddle and very active with working and caring for her aged parents, Jack himself found it harder and harder to get around.

So at the age of fifty, Sally had started a whole new career. Initially as a cook and domestic with the Department of Community Welfare, then as a residential care worker. The education Sally received through the Department was all paid for, in fact, she was paid to undertake it. Anyone who was willing to look after these children deserved all the help the government could afford. Sadly, there were never enough people. Or, there was never enough money. But she learnt a lot. One of the hardest things was that she would be expected to offer care and understanding to children who experienced trauma and difficult situations. She would be working with social workers, psychologists and other professionals to ensure the children received comprehensive care. And she would be working with children who were physically and mentally disabled.

Her training complete, Sally was assigned to a home that cared for about six children, all of whom had varying degrees of mental and physical disability. The house was an old federation house in Glenelg. There were many older style, large houses in Adelaide and those purchased by the government were fitted out to support the needs of their residents. Some retained gardens, but most of the blocks were given over to building additions, car spaces, bus spaces and occasional outbuildings. Sally thrived in her role. It was shift work of-course. The children had to be attended to 24 hours a day. She was often the only Residential

Care Worker but there were other staff in attendance during the day. One bedroom/office was set up for the person who would be on-call during the night. They called this a passive shift, but it was rarely passive. Sally would proudly take her adult children to the home when they visited from interstate, as Marie sometimes did or Lizzy if she showed an interest. George called in often but Billy rarely. Though he did know about his mother's work and could even deduce how much she loved it and, dare he say, loved some of the children in her care. Sally's old boss Mary had been correct. Sally did have the kind of compassion which suited her to looking after these very special children.

CHAPTER 27

Jack's passing

As well as being a dreamer, Jack was an innocent. The whole no sex before marriage thing bore this out to his two daughters. It was never discussed, but at thirty four when he married Sally, he was indeed a virgin. When the "long haired git" asked his permission to marry his youngest daughter, (yes the git had good manners and could play a decent game of chess) perhaps it was just the long hair which was disconcerting, he gave his permission, but said 'There must be no sex before the wedding'. Well, of course there already had been, and would continue to be at every opportunity the young people got. His innocence showed in other areas too. He watched the ABC news every day on television. He read the Advertiser from front to back every day. He was quite politically aware.

He had served in a war and lived through a depression. He had seen his father marry three times and both his in-laws marry twice. His favourite cousin, a farmer in the south east near Mt Gambier, had eleven children and some of those children got up to all sorts of mischief, and sadly, one had been killed in a motorbike accident. None of these world or local events made him "worldly". Nothing outside his own immediate family was of concern to him. He didn't learn anything from it. He ignored the fact that his continued coughing and pipe smoker might be related. He did know however, that his ill-health was getting to be a bit more than a temporary setback. He continued to tell his children 'When I get better I'll do such and such'. Every time Sally left for work he would answer her usual question of 'Are you all right Dear? Is there something I can get you?' with a smile and a kiss and 'I'm absolutely fine. See you when you get home'. Such a routine these two had. He did realise by now that he was sick. And yes, he was probably dying. Bad things did not happen to members of his family. He had no intention of leaving Sally alone. But he knew deep down, that this would eventually happen. The loss of Sharon was an unfortunate event, but life had gone on and now there were five grandchildren from

Marie and George. He hoped that Lizzy and Jeffrey left it a while before having children. They had already been separated for a few months and reunited. But Liz was still so young. Billy hadn't settled down yet. What was wrong with that boy? No, he was a bit tired and walking too far was a strain, but there was nothing seriously wrong with his health! At least, that is what he told his children.

Perhaps it wasn't innocence. Perhaps it was denial.

In July 1978 Sally eventually got him to go to a doctor. He was scheduled for surgery immediately. He told Lizzy, who by now lived in Adelaide and was a regular Sunday visitor to her parents, that they might take a lung. Not a problem, thought Lizzy. He's got two. He will be fine. Lizzy still adored her father and in her mind he would live forever. But she knew he was looking rather poorly. Silly old bugger should give up that pipe.

After the operation Jack's standard response to his children was. 'Everything was fine. They didn't take anything out. I'll have to have a bit of ray treatment though'.

In late August Lizzy organised a family get together at her and Jeffrey's place in Adelaide. Billy was coming and her grandparents. August was the month both Sally and Lizzy celebrated their birthdays. When Lizzy was on the phone a week earlier, arranging things with her mum, Sally suddenly realised that Lizzy did not know what was happening to her father.

'Lizzy, you know that this treatment your dad's having will only keep him going for another couple of years?' No. Lizzy did not know. She too was an innocent when it came to her father. She crumbled. Jeffrey had never seen her so upset. Did he know? Did the rest of the family know? Why hadn't anyone told her? Her Dad had told her he was OK!

The family BBQ went ahead as planned. For the first time Lizzy saw her father differently. We won't have him at Christmas. She thought to herself.

At the time Marie and her family were living in Melbourne. They came over to Adelaide a couple of time to see Jack. He was sitting in his chair at home, still smoking, still coughing. The next time they came over he was in hospital and Marie walked straight past him because she did not recognise him.

George and Georgie were on an overseas holiday in the September. They were still living in Mt Gambier at the time. Sally and Jack were looking after their two young children in their unit in Adelaide. But late in

September Sally sent the children back to Mt Gambier and Georgie's parents. George and his wife made an abrupt end to their holiday and rushed back to Australia and saw Jack late September.

Lizzy and her husband and Bill were living in Adelaide. Sally had Jack admitted to hospital in early September, but brought him home for a weekend. She was terrified. Lying in their double bed too scared to reach out and touch him. She knew that when she took him back to hospital the next day that she did not have the strength to bring him home again.

At the end of September Liz's husband and her brother took her to the hospital to see Jack. If she did not have those men with her, she too would have walked straight past him. Surely this withered, tiny man who could not even speak, was not her father. But it was.

Jack died a week later in October.

CHAPTER 28

After the Fact

Sally was only fifty-six years old when her husband died. Many years later, as each of her daughters reached that age themselves, they realised how young that was. And the boys, when they turned sixty-nine, breathed a sigh of relief that they had got past that terrible age. As children, even as adult children, we tend to think that our parents are incredibly old, but they will never die. How wrong we are. On both counts.

To say that Sally missed her husband is an understatement. She had known him for fifty years. By many standards of bereaved women, her thirty-five years of marriage was relatively short. For women of her time, that was thirty five years of domination by her partner. No matter that she loved him dearly, most of the time, she was still dominated by him. No matter that her children would willingly say that Mum was the boss, he still dominated her even if he didn't always dominate the family. There was no question of his love for her. He had loved her probably for those fifty years, in one form or another. He picked her out as his future wife when she was just a girl, not giving her a chance to experience more of life. He was a kind man, a gentle lover, a good father and quite possibly her best friend. But he did dominate her. This was a failing on Jack's part, but not necessarily his fault entirely. It was just how society was. It was a man's world and there was no escaping it. The only women who were not dominated by a man were those who had never married. She had three aunts who had never married, and two more who were widowed early and never re-married. These were strong, independent women with either careers, or callings of their own. There was a teacher, a nurse, and a banker. Her two aunts who were her father's sisters did not have careers as such, but were devoted to their charitable callings. What was she? Could she call her job with the Department of Community Welfare a Career? Some of her children certainly did. But her own self esteem didn't stretch that far. How could she be a career woman? She really had no ambition further than doing the best she could in the position she now had. The role of "wife" was now gone. The role of "mother" still remained, but was not highly appreciated by her very different and very independent children. She supposed she had done a good job in that regard, although the youngest one still caused her grief and would continue to for many years to come. And now there were five grandchildren with room for plenty more from her two youngest who had not yet reproduced. God she hoped Lizzy and Jeffrey did not have any babies. That marriage was doomed to failure. They had reconciled after a nine months breakup. They seemed happy enough, but she knew things were not right. Sally knew a lot of things were not right. She knew that Marie was unhappy, that Lizzy was unfaithful, that George suffered from his time in Vietnam and that Billy was a selfish little bastard but no one seemed to mind. He was still everyone's favourite, including hers.

But life must go on. And it did.

Her constants were her work and her Church. Unfortunately her own parents, that is, her mother and step father took up a lot of her time. She now did their house work, washing and took her mother shopping. Her mother had never been particularly fond of

Jack. The feeling was mutual, but she was devastated that he had passed away before her. There was only ten years difference in their age but Mabel still thought it very unfair that Sally lose her husband while she still had hers. Reg was about three years younger than Mabel and in fact he and Jack had been good mates. Often drinking together at their respective salesmen's clubs in Adelaide back in the day.

Church had become more of a social thing for Sally. Though, she did note that although she contributed more than what she considered her fare share to helping others, no-one from Church seemed to care about her. Certainly no one visited, except the minister, on rare occasions. Sally really didn't have any friends from Church. Why did she continue to attend? Habit she guessed.

There was one good friend, who had been a neighbour at one time in the block of units where she lived. Elly had been widowed a couple of years before Sally, and had moved to a different home, but she and Sally remained good friends for the rest of Elly's life.

Apart from that, there was work. Those poor kids that she was looking after. Sally put her heart and soul into those children. Hardly anyone called her Sally now. Most of her colleagues only knew her as Meredith and a handful of acquaintances she had didn't know her by the name that Jack had given her all those years ago. She only ever introduced herself as Meredith these days. What's in a name? Everything. Many years down the track, Lizzy changed her name by deed poll. She was hence forth known as Elizabeth Mary. No last name. Sally was offended when this was announced.

'Why don't you revert to your father's name?' she asked her youngest.

'Mum, no one knows me by that name anymore. I gave it up when I was eighteen. I have taken on three different surnames since then. I will never take on another man's name. Besides, if you look at my birth certificate you will see that my name is Elizabeth Mary. It doesn't even say my name is Saunders.' It was true. The South Australian Birth Certificate gave the names of both parents, but the child only has the given names.

It took Sally a while, but she did understand eventually. A name is really the only thing a woman has that is their very own. Why should they trade one man's name for another just because they get married, or divorced, or married again? And besides, it was Lizzy's father who gave her those two Christian names. In the end, Sally saw it as a way of Lizzy honouring her dad.

Sally was grateful that she had full time work to occupy her. In Adelaide at the time there was only Billy, who never came to see her. And Lizzy, who always feared her mother's disapproval, was afraid to visit very often. George and his family were still in Mt Gambier. Marie and her family were in Melbourne. Her relationship with Lizzy had always been tenuous, but for a while there they found some common ground. True to Sally's intuition Lizzy's marriage floundered a second time and both women found themselves without partners. Sally would sometimes call in to Lizzy's house after a shift, as it was much closer to her work than her unit south of Adelaide.

'Next time I'm going to find a younger man.' Sally announced one evening as they were enjoying a brandy and dry together. Lizzy was shocked. She could not imagine her mother having another man in her life. Why would she even think that? But she replied.

'Me too.' Jeffrey was nine years her senior. She had just always been attracted to older men and there was nothing Sally could say about it.

Sally did meet someone a few years later. There was a councillor who worked for the Department whom she had known for a number of years. They often crossed paths at regional meetings or training sessions or such events. Sally was approaching sixty and the man in question was a rather good looking fifty eight years old. He had the fortune of silver hair, not grey. Still stood tall but not imposing. On this particular occasion they had just finished a regional assessment meeting held at one of the Department office buildings. Everyone was packing away the chairs as was the norm after such talkfests.

'Would you like to have a drink now that the meeting is over?' asked Roger. He was a handsome man and Sally had most definitely noticed him when she first met him three years earlier. She supposed she had a bit of a crush on him. Very strange feeling that. She had never had a crush on anyone in her life. She had heard a lot of the teenagers she cared for at various time express this phenomenon, and she knew about school girl crushes on singers and movie stars. But for her to have a little flutter of the heart herself was most unusual.

'OK.' she replied. 'It is still early. I just don't want to be driving into the sun on my way home.' Sally was always a very practical person.

They drove separately to a hotel in Glenelg. One of those old colonial places on the beach. They enjoyed a drink together, but the "flutter" was no longer there. I don't want a lover. I just want a friend. Sally thought to herself, and that was the message she conveyed to Roger. In 1989 she heard a new song with exactly those words. It was not often played on the radio station she listened to, so she secretly bought the album by Texas. Every time she played it she had a little smile to herself. The interlude was good for her ego. It showed that she was attractive to the opposite sex. Something which she had never considered previously.

Roger continued to be her friend. Sally never told any of her children of this incident. To them she was just mum. The thought of her partnering up with anyone was abhorrent.

Sally bought a little red car. She had the cash and the inclination. It was the first new car she had ever known. She and Jack had only ever had second hand cars. She knew exactly what she wanted. A Datsun Sunny. The car salesman was a little surprised to see this mature woman come into the showroom on her own and be so specific about what she wanted. She would not be drawn to any other model and she would not be drawn into taking out finance. The deal was almost done when the salesman discovered that the only colour readily available was red.

'That will do just fine.' Sally said. She could hardly control her grin. She couldn't wait to show her ultra conservative oldest child what she had bought.

George loved it. 'About time you got something for yourself Mum.' was his reaction. That boy was a wonder. Just when she thought she had him all worked out he would say something completely unexpected like that.

Sally continued to work full time until she was 65 years old. She was officially "retired" from the Department at sixty, but they continued to employ her as a relief worker. Which meant things continued just the same as before except she was paid more. Eventually the powers that be had to stop rostering her on as it went against some bureaucratic rule. In the mean time however, Sally had saved up a nice little sum and decided to go on an overseas trip. She had never been outside of Australia previously, not even to Tasmania.

She lived on her own, so there were no arguments or debating as to where she would go. She did all the research herself. Bought all the required tickets, then told her children.

'Who are you travelling with?' they each asked when told of her plans.

'No-one. I'm going by myself. There are a couple of Group Tours in the mix, but there will also be weeks on end when I will explore by myself.'

'Good on you' was the general reply. She didn't need the approval of her children, but it was nice to have their support in this venture.

Sally returned after three months with a folder full of brochures and photos and postcards. She had a wonderful time. Her only complaint was sharing a room on the group tour with a woman who snored. Sally had got used to not sharing a room, or anything for that matter, with anyone. It certainly made the decision making process easier whenever there was a decision in her life to be made. She had never really been a single person before. She quite liked it.

Being a single, mature woman does not guarantee immediate respect by all members of society. It was Sally's habit to walk to the local shops rather than drive. She was returning across a nearby parklands one Saturday afternoon. The parkland was really just a broad section of lawn and a pathway running between two roads which ran horizontal to each other. She was clearly a solitary figure. An old lady of average height and a little stooped. Handbag over the shoulder. From habit, it was also clutched in her left hand in front of her body. She had a shopping bag in her right hand. She heard running footsteps approaching from behind and then a sudden strong tug on her handbag. Up goes the left elbow as she swivelled around.

'What did you do that for?' she exclaimed to the youth who had made a grab for her handbag. He was clearly not expecting such a reaction and ran off. Groceries were spread around her, but the handbag was still in her possession. She gathered up her strewn items and continued home. A nice cup of tea was in order. But what she did was sit in Jack's old chair and cry for about an hour. She was in shock, but not injured. The incident would play over and over again in her mind for many years.

Soon after that, Sally got a dog.

Missy was a black and white Shelty breed. She looked just like Prince the Border Collie, only smaller. When her first two children were very young Prince appeared from nowhere and saved her from emotional fatigue. Missy saved her from loneliness. They went everywhere together. She travelled across the country in the little red car when the children spread themselves out over the land. The dog even travelled by airplane a few times. When Sally went to visit her children, which she did every year no matter where they lived, house rules were changed so that Missy would be welcomed.

When one gets to be past seventy years old, friends and relations start to fall off the perch. Her father had died quite young and one of her brothers also when only fifty-eight years old. Both her father's sisters had passed. Mr and Mrs Wright both lived to see eighty before they died and her own mother was eighty-two when she passed. Two of her mother's sisters were past the century when they eventually passed. Sally hoped that that was not a genetic thing. She did not want to be a "little doll, just laying there" as was one of these aunts. Eventually her brother Peter passed and her step-father. He was only five years older than Jack but lived fifteen years longer. With the passing of her step-father came an inheritance. It was not a huge amount, but it was enough to allow Sally to purchase her own home. She and Jack had bought houses on a couple of occasions, but they were always mortgaged. So, at the age of seventy-two Sally bought a house in the neighbouring suburb to the unit she had rented for fifteen years. The house hunting didn't take very long. She was quite adamant that she wanted to stay in the same area, close to her Church and the few friends she had made. By this time, she was driving for Meals on Wheels plus other community services. Sally was part of the community of that area in southern Adelaide and wanted to stay there. George was the only one of her children who still lived in the capital. Unfortunately, he lived as far north as she did south. But she was not to be deterred. Sally would tell the story many times 'As soon as I walked inside this house, I knew it was for me.' It took her no time at all to make the three bedroom house comfortable, just for her. And the garden! Well, it was three times as big as the one she had at the unit. It was amazing what that woman could do with a bit of dirt and some elbow grease.

It was a long widowhood and Sally's children were the centre of her life. But of-course, she was not the centre of their lives. There were four more grandchildren now. But they were so spread out over the country. Besides, Sally was not a doting grandma. She had never been an affectionate woman but her children were used to that. A kiss hello and a kiss goodbye was all they expected. The grandchildren treated her with respect but did not expect to be spoiled like some of their friends were spoiled by their grandparents. Sally always tried to impart wisdom to her grandchildren rather than unrealistic fantasy.

There were fallings out between Sally and each of her children.

With George it was over where she should live. He was the only one left in Adelaide at the time Sally bought her house and thought she should choose somewhere closer to him and his family. It was a long drive to see her on a regular basis. She could come and have meals with them. He could help her in the garden if she was closer. They could take her shopping if need be as she grew older. Lots of reasons, in George's mind why his mother should move closer to him. For Sally's part, she did not expect him to visit on a weekly basis. She had never felt particularly comfortable in George's house. She thought his wife bossed him around too much, though she would never say this to him. She was quite capable of making changes to her garden herself thank you very much and she was also quite capable of doing her own shopping. If she became decrepit enough to need help she would get it from the same service she currently gave help to!

For Marie it was lots of things. They wasted money on a business venture that didn't turn out right. Bob could never settle at the right job after leaving the army. They got all involved in Amway. They got all involved in some other "life affirming" marriage counselling. They were too obsessed with each other – what about the kids? Marie was not a very good housekeeper. They would just buy a beautiful home and then a couple of years later sell it and move on. Nothing Marie did seemed to meet with her mother's approval. In the end, she just stopped trying. It was her husband who pointed out to Marie that some mothers are just never happy with their children. It didn't mean she loved her daughter any less. She was the same with all four of her children. She loved them, Bob was certain of it, Sally just didn't know how to show it.

Billy was a bit of a flippertyjibbit. But basically, the sun shone out of his backside. She must have had a few words to say about something though because of the finger wagging incident. Sally would always remember that. And wonder what it was that she did wrong. Billy was very lax in phone calls and visits. He never wrote when he and his family moved to Perth. He lived in the Solomon Islands for a year or so, with his wife, before they had their two sons. Sally went over to visit them there. Sally went wherever her children were to visit them at least once a year. At one time Marie was in Queensland, Billy in Perth and Lizzy in Wollongong. George was always in Adelaide. He was her rock.

Lizzy. Shall we talk about Lizzy? Probably best not to. Sally certainly didn't talk to any of her friends about Lizzy. How could they be expected to keep up with who was her latest husband! She'd married the "long haired git" when she was eighteen. Then there was the alcoholic twenty four years her senior. That man was unemployed and drunk on their wedding day, she was sure of it. And it didn't get any better despite the two beautiful children they produced. The next husband tried to impress Sally with his wealth. Nothing impressed Sally and definitely not how much money he said he had. It only took Lizzy two years to work out that one was a big mistake. Fortunately, Lizzy did eventually find Mr Wonderful after she had packed up her children and moved to Perth (Why not to Adelaide where her mother lived?). When Sally met Liz's new partner, she told Billy she wished Lizzy had met him twenty years ago. So did Lizzy.

CHAPTER 29

In the end

When Sally was seventy-eight she was a very fit old lady. The last cigarette was some fifty years ago, and even then it was only ever menthol. She did enjoy a brandy and dry of an evening, but only ever one unless someone was visiting. The sherry bottle was only replaced about every three months or so. She would walk down to the local shop every day to buy the paper, and take Missy for her exercise. Every morning she had a routine of exercises even before she got out of bed. She had learnt this routine when she was working for the Department. A physiotherapist had given a class on exercises for the bed ridden or some such thing. She would work her way down her body, starting at her neck and ending with her toes. Contracting and releasing each set of muscles five times.

It would take about half an hour, but seeing she woke at 5am every morning it was not an intrusion on her day. She did this without fail every morning. She was also a stickler for healthy food. Salad for lunch every day, lots of celery. She still enjoyed cooking, although she admitted she was not particularly adventurous. A casserole would always be a stew of some sort. Pasta was spaghetti for goodness sake. Potatoes should always be boiled to death. Sauté meant simmer. A roast was a roast in anyone's language and steak was only eaten by rich people. She still cooked for two but froze half for later.

So, when she was diagnosed with ovarian cancer it was quite a shock for everyone.

'What are they going to do?' asked Marie and Lizzy. All frowns and conjecture. At least this time someone had used the "C" word which was never used in their father's case.

'Nothing they can do really.' replied Sally. She seemed rather too disinterested for the girls' liking.

'What! Just because you're seventy-eight they think you are too old to worry about. Don't they know how fit you are?' the daughters protested.

As it turned out Sally's GP did know how fit she was and referred her to a different surgeon. This delightful young man was prepared to operate and then follow up with chemotherapy. Sally's GP was happy with that, and so was everyone else.

The operation went well. The chemo was only for six months and one of the children made sure they were there with her in hospital when it happened. Lizzy and Billy took turns coming over from Perth and Marie came from Queensland.

Shortly after the chemo, Sally was back on the road again. The little red car had met with an accident and was replaced with a Subaru. A manual, much to everyone's chagrin, but Sally loved it. For the next four years life was as it had been previously. Sally continued to drive across the country until George eventually talked her into giving up her license at eighty-two. Sadly, Missy was now buried in the back yard and would not be replaced.

In these last five years of her life Sally eventually "mellowed". Her grandchildren still held her in awe, but were no longer afraid of her. Lizzy had forgiven her all the things she thought her mother had done wrong and Sally had forgiven Lizzy all the things she thought she had done wrong. Marie still had a few issues which she never really did get to sort out with her mother. But in the end, she knew her mum was a good sort and had probably suffered from depression for much of her life. She remembered Sally being a member of a group called COPE. It was hard to get the gist of it, but apparently Sally was not coping very well with many things, at various times, and she sort help from other people in similar situations. Still, the word depression, was never used.

George increased his visits to his mother but she rarely went to visit him. She did worry that he was drinking too much red wine though. But didn't say anything, not to George anyway. And Billy. Well, he had never caused her a bad day in his life and now he had two wonderful little boys of his own.

Early in 2006 Sally was sitting in her usual chair in her lounge room enjoying the cricket on TV as was her favourite pastime. Suddenly she felt incredibly unwell. She tried to get up to go to the bathroom, but couldn't. She felt like she was painfully constipated. But she didn't have the strength to get up. She was shocked. Yesterday she was coping quite well. A few more Panamax than usual and yes, constipation was becoming a frequent problem. She had put up with chemotherapy four years ago, but mostly because she believed it would give her extra time. And it had. What was happening now? Suddenly she became afraid. Alone and afraid. She called George.

He was there within an hour. Good driving from where he lived on the other side of town. He took one look at her, or rather, Georgie, his wife did, and they ordered an ambulance immediately. Sally was taken to the Repatriation hospital in Adelaide. The very hospital that she had worked in all those years ago. And, the one in which her Jack had died. Sally was an ex-service woman herself and was entitled to this care.

Things were not looking good. Billy and Liz flew over from Perth. Marie flew down from Queensland. Someone suggested that they put a whole lot of photos on Sally's bed table depicting all the grandchildren. She had barely been conscious since arriving in hospital five days earlier. All four were gathered around her bed when suddenly Sally opened her eyes. Struggling up on her pillow she declared

'What is all this in aid of?' indicating the photos. 'What are you all doing here?'

What could they say? There was much mollifying and hugs and congratulations for looking so good. We were worried there for a minute, etc. etc. etc.

'Well, I'm not dead yet.' She declared. And she wasn't.

Everyone went home to their own states and families. Sally stayed in hospital for a few more weeks. She was obliged to undergo some remedial therapy to see if she could look after herself at home.

'They wanted me to make scones, for heaven's sake.' She told Billy over the phone. 'I told them I've been making scones since I was ten years old. Showed them a thing or two about cooking as well.'

Sally was well and truly back in the land of the living. She was allowed to go home. She was allowed to live by herself. There was now a constant flow of phone calls from all over the country and George and Georgie were regular callers. They assisted with shopping, checking that meals were prepared and so on. Sally was already getting some help from the local community welfare people by way of housework and a shower every other day. But really, it was the cups of tea and chats which she enjoyed the most. True to her word, she whispered to herself, 'I told George I didn't need his help. That I would get it from the people I used to volunteer for myself.'

But she did need George's help. The next attack came four months later. And this time they did not let her go home to live alone.

Everything was arranged very quickly. Too quickly. A place was found for her in an aged care facility (near George). Her house was sold to pay for it. She was moved from her lovely little house to a room! She was not happy.

'I just want to go home.' She told Lizzy.' But I know the house has been sold.'

'Have you met any new people Mum? At meal times and in the garden.' enquired Lizzy. She was not going to dwell on what could no longer be for her mother. But she did try to sound positive.

'It's a brand new complex.' replied Sally. There is hardly anyone here. They bring my meals to my room. I can't really get out of bed. And they wont let me have even a box of Panamax in my room. If I want one, I have to push a button and wait for someone to come.' Lizzy was horrified at that. But 'them's the rules' in a place which is supposed to be a person's final "home" before they die. Fortunately, George came every day and they shared a glass of brandy and dry together.

'I wish you had just left me there in the chair'. She told George one day. She was very angry indeed. But not really with George. She was more angry at herself for calling him. She could have passed there in her own chair in her own home and been quite happy about it. But of course, the natural state of the human is to survive. And to fight for survival.

Sally's life did not flash before her eyes as she died. Sadly, it was a slow and uncomfortable death. Her body had collapsed and only her brain remained active. And because she was pumped full of so many pain relief drugs she could not really communicate with those around her. She knew they were there though. Saying nice things and telling her how much they loved her. Really, it was all a bit tiresome and she would sometimes pretend to be asleep when she wasn't. Only Lizzy knew when her mother was "foxing", but didn't tell the others.

Sally smiled at Lizzy, who had given her the most trouble. It was strange that she was the child who ended up living on a farm, surrounded by animals and loving it, just as Sally herself loved that life in Melrose. And there was Billy. She still remembered the finger wagging incident and it made her smile. That she, an old lady, should be telling her grown-up son what to do, and he told her off for wagging her finger at him.

There was George with his Georgina. George had done everything right in his life. She was so proud of him. She was sorry that she had not warmed to Georgina because it was so obvious that the woman loved her oldest son as much as Jack had loved her. And her poor Marie. She was so sorry that she could not spend more time with her when her little girl died. It was Sally's only regret, and in a moment of lucidness she managed to tell Marie this.

People said that she would see little Sharon and her Jack again after she passed on. But she didn't really believe that. There were an awful lot of people "up there" that she didn't particularly want to see again. She rather liked the stories that old Willy-Jack had told her of the Dreamtime Creation, much better than the Book of Genesis. Sally believed that when you died, you were gone. So you had better make the most of life while you had it and be grateful. But she did wish she and Jack had more time together. She knew he loved her with all his heart. She knew he adored her. She knew that she could never have found another man who would suit her so well. She remembered the way he looked right inside her, to her soul, (She did believe in souls but just didn't know what happened to them after you died). She remembered the way he would draw her into his arms and take away all fear and pain and worry. In the last year of his life, when Jack was sitting in his chair at home, he pulled Sally onto his lap. He kissed her on the lips and said 'I love you Sally'. It made her cry then and the memory of it made her cry now.

Sally survived till July of that year. And then she left. She was just shy of eighty-four years old.

Acknowledgements

My deepest thanks to Sally's children for their memories. Particularly the oldest child, represented as George in this story.

Thanks too to two of the children of Sally's youngest brother. Their research into the descendants of Robert Thomas and George Napier Burk is much appreciated.

To my friend Helen Silver who read my manuscript with red pen in hand. Spell check really only goes so far but a knowledge of good grammar is essential. As a writer, one misses so much in the hast to get it all down. Thank you for your time and encouragement Helen.

My fellow readers from the Saturday Book Club in my local town did some workshopping with me on the first draft, I appreciate their comments and suggestions.

To my husband, children, brothers and sisters and friends who knew about this, my first major writing project, thank you for your love and support.

About the author

Katherine Jane was raised in South Australia, had her children in New South Wales, and moved to Western Australia in the late 1990s. With a background in finance and administration, she and her husband spent fifteen years building, running, and marketing a successful farmstay business in York, Western Australia.

Katherine's debut novel, Sally, is set in South Australia, though it could just as easily have taken place in the wheatbelt of Western Australia, where many soldier settlers were sent to carve out a living on the land.

After selling their small farm and accommodation business, Katherine and her husband retired in 2023. She now enjoys a quieter life south of Perth in a place the locals call paradise, where her days revolve around reading, writing, daily exercise, and embracing the peace of her surroundings.